Daddys howse

Lake

Daddy

Me!

by Tyler Montgumry, age 4½

ABOUT THE AUTHOR

Emily Dalton has loved romance since she first read *Pride and Prejudice* and *Jane Eyre*. When it occurred to her that it might be fun to write her own romances, she began with several Regencies and historicals. Now she concentrates on contemporary romances for Harlequin American Romance, and this year won *Romantic Times Magazine*'s Reviewers' Choice Award for Best Harlequin American Romance of 1997, *Wake Me with a Kiss*.

With three boys at home, none of whom are quite grown up yet—including her husband!—she enjoys juggling her career with homemaking and motherhood. Besides writing, Emily loves to travel, read other people's books, take long walks and eat chocolate truffles.

Books by Emily Dalton

HARLEQUIN AMERICAN ROMANCE

586—MAKE ROOM FOR DADDY
650—HEAVEN CAN WAIT
666—ELISE & THE HOTSHOT LAWYER
685—WAKE ME WITH A KISS
706—MARLEY AND HER SCROOGE
738—DREAM BABY
750—SIGN ME, SPEECHLESS IN SEATTLE

Instant Daddy

EMILY DALTON

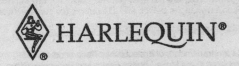

HARLEQUIN®

TORONTO • NEW YORK • LONDON
AMSTERDAM • PARIS • SYDNEY • HAMBURG
STOCKHOLM • ATHENS • TOKYO • MILAN • MADRID
PRAGUE • WARSAW • BUDAPEST • AUCKLAND

To my sisters in Alaska, Cyndi Romberg
and Cheri Woods
I'll always have wonderful memories and a grateful heart
for the years we lived together as a family.
Love you,
Danice

ISBN 0-373-16783-0

INSTANT DADDY

Chapter One

"Here, Cass. Check this out. Maybe you'll find your dream man in Alaska."

Cassie automatically caught the magazine Susan tossed from halfway across the bookstore. She glanced at the periodical, its glossy cover showing a grinning hunk of guy in a red flannel shirt and tight jeans against a backdrop of majestic mountain peaks. When she read the title, *Single Men of Alaska,* she immediately set it aside on a nearby table and returned to her job of unpacking magazines and arranging them on shelves.

"The store opens in twenty minutes, Susan. I don't have time—*we* don't have time to goof around. There are still three boxes full of women's magazines to set out for display."

"All work and no play makes Cass a dull girl," Susan retorted. "Aren't you even tempted to check out all the cute guys advertising for companionship from the icy back of beyond?"

Cassie turned and threw her friend a rueful grin. "If they have to advertise, I can't imagine that they're any great catch."

Susan shook her head vigorously, the chestnut brown curls bouncing against her cheeks. "That's where you're wrong, Cass. These guys advertise for the simple reason that there's about five times as many men in Alaska as women." She moved to the table where Cassie had put down the magazine on a stack of *Cosmo*'s. She picked it up and flipped through a few pages, then shoved the open magazine to within two inches of Cassie's face. "Do these guys look like losers to you?"

Cassie gave an exasperated laugh, took the magazine and sat down on the edge of the table. "All right. If it will get you off my back and back to work, I'll look. But only for a minute. Besides, aren't you forgetting that I've got a boyfriend?"

Susan crossed her arms over her chest and snorted. "I suppose you mean Brad?"

"Who else? We've been dating for two years, haven't we?"

"That's exactly my point. Dating but not *mating*. You two haven't even slept together."

Cassie felt herself blushing. "Susan, you know I don't believe in rushing things. I'd like to be sure of my feelings for Brad before we get intimate."

"I understand why you feel that way, Cass. I mean, after what happened to you..." Susan's words trailed off.

Cassie said nothing. Susan, and just about all her other friends, thought that what had happened to her five years ago was the worst thing that could happen to any young woman. Cassie didn't agree, but there was no point in arguing.

After a tactful pause, Susan continued persistently. "But I still don't see how you can date a guy for two years and abstain from sex the whole time unless something's just not clicking between you. Face the facts, ma'am. You're *never* going to be sure about Brad. In all fairness you should either make a commitment to the poor guy or give him his walking papers and let him get on with his life. Sometimes I think you just use your relationship with Brad as an excuse not to get involved with anyone you might *really* fall in love with."

Susan's lecture was interrupted by the phone's ringing. She gave Cassie one last admonishing glance and went to answer it.

Cassie hung her head and thumbed idly through the magazine. Though she'd muttered under her breath a time or two, Susan had never before spoken so forcefully on the subject of Cassie's ambiguous relationship with Brad. She herself had never considered the possibility that she was using him, and she'd certainly never consciously done so. She cared about Brad, *only*...

Susan was right about one thing. The guy deserved to know where he stood. She really should make a decision one way or the other about Brad. But every time he tried to get close, every time marriage crept into the conversation, she got cold feet.

There was certainly nothing wrong with Brad Callahan. In fact, he was a great guy. He was good-looking, kind and loving, and wasn't too shabby as a cowboy-cum-businessman, either. After all, he'd taken a small, struggling cattle ranch he'd inherited from his uncle three years ago and turned it into a thriving concern.

Brad's ranch was five miles outside of town, just down the road from Cassie's home, the much larger spread owned and operated by her father, Jasper Montgomery. As neighbors do in the mostly rural Big Sky country of Montana, Brad and Jasper spoke over the fence while straddling their horses and eventually became good friends as the older cowboy shared his years of ranching experience with the novice. Now Brad was more like a son than a neighbor to Jasper, and nothing would make both of them happier than for Cassie to formalize the connection by saying "I do."

Jasper's wholehearted endorsement wasn't the only one. Tyler adored Brad. However, Cassie felt her barely four-year-old son was too young to be clearheaded in his judgment, particularly about a man who carried Jolly Rancher candies in his pocket and wasn't ashamed to use them as bribes.

Cassie felt her heart swell with love at the thought of the most important "man" in her life. Tyler might be a mistake in the eyes of most of the residents of the tiny town of Nye, Montana, where she was born and raised and now ran a combination bookstore-coffee bar called The Buzz, but Cassie could never regret the night of passion that had brought Tyler into the world nine months later.

No, even if Tyler hadn't been the result of that night of indiscretion, Cassie couldn't bring herself to regret the most incredibly romantic experience of her life....

She'd been barely twenty. She and three of her girlfriends had gone to the annual Fourth of July fair sponsored by the local cattle ranchers and town merchants. Nye had retained a lot of rough-and-tumble ambiance from the first rush of miners who came in droves when ore was first discovered in the surrounding mountainsides in the last century, and summer brought a fair number of tourists to enjoy that ambiance.

They'd gaze up at the angular, painted timber buildings that still stood along Main Street, buildings that used to be mostly saloons, but which now housed antique shops, candy stores and restaurants, including Cassie's bookstore.

So, when Cassie and her friends were strolling along the grassy fairway, eating pink cotton candy, they weren't surprised to see a lot of strange faces in the crowd. But when a certain face turned in their direction and a handsome young man disengaged himself from the surrounding people, walked deliberately up to them and began a conversation, they were awestruck. Nye had rarely seen the likes of this guy. With his chiseled face and devastating smile, his dark hair and sky-blue eyes, he was movie-star gorgeous.

He told them he was just passing through town at the end of a short course of summer college classes. He was staying at Cavana House, the bed-and-breakfast run by Mr. and Mrs. Tuddenham, and he'd been excited to find out there was a fair in town. Would they tell him which of the animal exhibitions were the best, and which concessions stand had the spiciest hot dogs? As he chatted about the town, the fair and the mild July weather, he oozed charm from every refined pore.

Jamie, the bravest and most flirtatious of their

group, invited him to tag along with them for the evening. He'd happily agreed. But as the evening wore on, Cassie found herself, rather than the forward Jamie, more and more the object of his interest. Cassie, bookish and shy, only pretty in a quiet sort of way with her straight blond hair, gray eyes and pale complexion, was more surprised by his interest in her than anyone else.

They rode together on the Ferris wheel. He knocked down bottles and won her a large stuffed Wile E. Coyote. They ate hot dogs and caramel apples, then nearly got sick on the merry-go-round. At the end of the ride when he lifted her off the aqua-blue horse with the gilded harness, dizzy and laughing, she felt a strong stirring of sexual desire the likes of which she'd never experienced before.

Later, while the other girls went home in Jamie's car, the handsome stranger walked Cassie to hers. She ended up giving him a ride to the bed-and-breakfast...then sneaking in with him and staying all night.

Nothing like this had ever happened to Cassie before. Up until that night, she'd been a virgin and with no great temptation to be anything else. But this stranger, this man who only wanted to be known by his fraternity nickname, "Bogie"—which he said had come about because of his rapt involvement in a Humphrey Bogart marathon on cable one year despite looming final exams—had swept her off her feet and into his bed by the sheer power of his considerable charisma.

In the wee hours of the morning, he walked her to her car, kissed her lingeringly through the open window, and made arrangements to meet her the following day for a picnic.

Giddy with excitement, Cassie prepared a basket of food and drove to the park where they were to tryst. After waiting an hour for him to show up, she went to the Cavana House to see what was keeping him. Mr. Tuddenham explained that "Mr. Bogart," which was the name he'd actually registered under, had received a long-distance call that morning and left in a great hurry.

Cassie was disappointed, but life went on and she would have tucked away her romantic memory of that night for the occasional indulgence of lazy afternoon daydreaming, if a month's worth of throwing up and a pregnancy test hadn't changed everything...changed her life forever.

"Cassie? Cassie, where are you, girl? By that grim look on your face, you must not like whoever you're reading about."

Susan snatched the magazine and stared at the page Cassie had randomly opened to.

"Oh my *gaw*... If you don't think *he's* cute, there's something definitely wrong with you, Cass. And what a neat name. Adam Baranof. Must be Russian. Didn't a bunch of them Tolstoy types settle in Alaska eons ago? Geez, he's even a marine biologist. Brainy *and* brawny. What more could you want?"

Cassie glanced down at the page Susan was waving under her nose. "I'm just not interested, Su—"

Cassie's heart stopped beating, then came to life again with a hard thump she felt clear to her toes.

"Cass? Cass, what's wrong? You look just like

my mom did when she got food poisoning after eating Aunt Ida's home-canned succotash. Are you gonna be sick?''

With trembling fingers, Cassie took the magazine out of Susan's hands and stared disbelievingly at the picture of a dark-haired man with sky-blue eyes. A man who was movie-star gorgeous.

''It's…it's *him.*''

''What do you mean *him?* Don't tell me you know this guy?''

Cassie nodded slowly. ''Oh, I know him all right.''

''As in the *biblical* sense you know him? But I thought the only guy you'd ever slept with was Tyler's—''

Susan fell silent. Cassie glanced up and saw her friend's mouth hanging open like a hungry baby bird's.

''Yes, it's Tyler's father, Susan,'' Cassie confirmed in a raspy voice. ''I thought I'd never be able to tell my son who his father is. But now I know.''

''Are…are you sure?''

''I could never forget that face.''

''I can see why.''

Now they both lapsed into stunned silence, staring at the picture of Adam Baranof.

Adam Baranof. Cassie thought the romantic name suited him…or at least suited the memory she had of him and of his suave charm. The ad seemed fitting, too. He wasn't advertising for a wife or a long-term relationship like some of the other men in the magazine. He was advertising for a *friend.* Someone to share a few good times with, a few laughs, a few walks on the beach. To the right woman he was willing to send a first-class airplane ticket for a weekend rendezvous in Alaska. Seldovia, Alaska, to be precise...wherever that was.

Cassie shook her head. After five years and several early and futile attempts to track down Tyler's father, she found it hard to believe that his identity could be revealed to her in this weird, accidental way.

"So now that you know, what are you going to do, Cass?"

Susan's softly spoken question was a good one.

"I...I don't know," Cassie answered. "I always thought he should know about Tyler. I didn't want or need financial support or anything, but it just seemed right to tell a man he'd become a father. But it's been so long since he was here. He might not remember me. He might not even *want* to know...you know?"

"Well, I think he *should* know," Susan stated, growing indignant as the shock wore off. "He obviously wasn't very careful that night or you wouldn't have gotten pregnant. And then he left town willy-nilly the next morning, leaving you to go through the whole ordeal alone."

"It wasn't an ordeal, Susan," Cassie reminded her in a firm tone. "I loved every minute I was pregnant with Tyler, and that little boy is the center of my universe."

"I know all that, Cass," Susan hastily assured her. "That's not what I meant. It's just that men shouldn't go around getting women pregnant, then taking no responsibility for it."

"He didn't know I was pregnant."

"Well, he sure as heck knew you could be, didn't he? It's one of the things that can happen when two people...you know...tango!"

"Neither of us thought about the possible consequences, Susan. Neither of us was careful. It was as much my doing as his." Cassie felt her cheeks glowing with warmth. "We were just sort of... *carried away* by our passions."

Susan grabbed Cassie by the shoulders and gazed intently into her face. "You still have the hots for this guy, don't you?"

Cassie shrugged, embarrassed and confused. "Of course not."

"But I'll bet you'll never forget that night *or* that man," Susan persisted.

"It *was* a pretty magical night. And he *was*—" Cassie shook her head, sighed and smiled "—pretty incredible."

"And pretty unforgettable. If that night was as great as you say, I'm sure he feels the same way about you."

"I doubt it," Cassie answered bluntly. "He didn't make any effort to contact me, did he? I apparently didn't make quite the same impression on him as he did on me."

"There's only one way to find out for sure," Susan suggested with a coyly raised brow.

Cassie stared suspiciously at her friend. "To find out *what* for sure?"

"If you made an impression on him. Answer his ad, Cassie. Send him a picture. You'll find out fast enough if he remembers you."

Trying to ignore the way her heart fluttered with excitement, Cassie paced the floor. "If I *were* to get in contact with Adam, my object wouldn't be to try to rekindle something between us. It would be to tell him about Tyler. That's all."

"But I thought you weren't sure if you *should* tell him about Tyler?"

"You're right. I'm *not* sure!"

Susan nodded sagely. "Well, I agree, you're right to be cautious. I mean, how much do you really know about this guy except that he's great in the sack?"

Cassie stopped pacing and whirled around to face her friend. "Susan! I know more than *that!*"

Now Susan raised both brows. "Oh, you do? *What* exactly? He left town without even telling you his real name. Did you know he was a scientist?"

Cassie frowned and shook her head. "No, but—"

"No buts. You really don't know this guy from Adam." Susan stopped abruptly and laughed at her own unintentional joke. "Seriously, Cass, what if he's really not a very nice man? What if he doesn't like kids? What if he *does* like them and wants Tyler to spend six months out of the year in Alaska?"

Now Cassie's heart fluttered with apprehension. "Are you trying to scare me, Susan?"

"No. All I'm saying is that you ought to get to know this guy before you tell him about Tyler."

"How am I supposed to do that?"

Susan sighed and raised both hands in the air.

"Answer the ad, Cass. Just answer the ad. It's that simple."

DRIVING HOME for lunch, as she passed through a flat stretch of grassland where range cows stood in the warm June sun and a loping coyote chased a field mouse across the road, Cassie thought about Susan's arguments for answering Adam's ad. Susan had made it sound simple, but it wasn't. It was complicated, and what complicated it the most was the person who mattered most in her life. Tyler.

Would he hold it against her someday if she decided not to contact his father when she had the chance? People moved around. If she didn't write to Adam now, he could disappear from their lives as quickly as he'd accidentally reappeared.

But contacting him could also possibly cause an upheaval in their lives they'd never recover from. What if he wanted to be part of Tyler's life? What if he wanted to be part of *her* life again?

Cassie pushed that idea out of her mind before the Cinderella scenario could take over and she started envisioning herself and Tyler snugly ensconced in some palatial log cabin in Alaska with a Russian prince.

Being part of a family, having more children with a man with whom you were at least on a first-name basis, was a dream she cherished. But such a dream seemed far more likely to come true with a stable man like Brad, who lived next door, than with a marine biologist advertizing for a "friend" in some remote town called Seldovia in faraway Alaska.

Cassie crossed the bridge over the fast-flowing Stillwater River and drove more quickly than usual through the open gate under the Lone Mountain Ranch sign that was suspended high above the dirt road from a rustic pine framework. Dust flew in the wake of her Subaru Outback, but she was eager to see Tyler and anxious to talk to her father about her incredible discovery.

She skidded to a stop in front of the fieldstone-and-log ranch house she called home, with the familiar forested mountains behind it and outbuildings of every size and variety scattered on the grounds around it. Tucking the *Single Men of Alaska* magazine under her arm, she stepped out of the car and trained her eyes on the front door.

She wasn't disappointed. The door flew open and Tyler flew out, his granddad following in long, lazy strides, making no attempt to keep up.

"Ty! How's my little cowboy?"

"Me and Granddad caught two trouts!" Tyler announced as his mother scooped him into her arms for a quick kiss and hug. "And Sylvie's cookin' 'em fer lunch!"

"That sounds delicious," Cassie said with enthusiasm, although with her stomach in such a nervous state she wasn't sure if she'd be able to eat a single bite. She smiled down at Tyler, marveling again—after seeing the photo of Adam—at how much he looked like his father. He had the same dark hair and blue eyes. And that dimple in his chin would undoubtedly grow into a cleft just like Adam's.

"Your foot was pressed to the metal comin' down the drive, hon," her father observed in his usual laconic drawl. "Did ya think ya saw smoke comin' from the house, or are ya just hungry?"

Cassie looked at her father, at his tall, rangy figure in jeans and a Levi's shirt, at the sun-weathered face and drooping gray mustache that made him look a little older than his fifty-seven years. Today there was a twinkle in his pale blue eyes, but they had blazed with anger five years ago when he'd found out some passer-through had impregnated his daughter, then flown the coop.

Time had worked its magic and he'd long ago come to terms with the way Tyler had become part of their lives. Now he was just grateful for his grandson, for the sheer pleasure and vitality he brought to their little family which had seemed so diminished after the death of Cassie's mother six years before.

Jasper spent a good part of his day with the boy, sharing the ups and downs of child-rearing with Cassie and their sixtyish nanny-housekeeper, Sylvie. The influence of a cattle-rancher grandfather was evident; Ty was only four but he already rode a horse and knew how to rope a steer. He wore his boots to bed—they had to be removed after he was asleep—and he didn't leave the house without his Stetson, grooved just so at the crown and curved at the brim just like Granddad's.

"No smoke. Just anxious to get home," Cassie replied with a smile as she held Tyler's hand and walked alongside her father to the door. Then, she added in a lowered voice, as Tyler hurried ahead to the kitchen toward the smell of fresh trout sizzling in the skillet, "Actually, there is something I need to talk to you about, Dad. Something important."

Her father's eyes narrowed and he looked at her keenly. "All right, hon. We'll talk after lunch when Sylvie puts Ty down for his nap. That all right?"

Cassie nodded and released a shaky sigh. "That would be perfect."

STANDING IN her father's study, which was paneled in warm, honeyed tones of knotty pine, with a huge trout hung over the mantel and copies of Remington sketches framed on the walls, Cassie watched Jasper Montgomery's face as he took his first look at Tyler's father. He wasn't smiling.

"So this is the scoundrel," he muttered.

"Dad, I thought you'd gotten over wanting to wring his neck!" Cassie exclaimed.

"I thought so, too. Guess I was wrong."

"As I've told you before, I was a consenting adult. In fact, I was more than willing."

Her father grimaced, then sighed. "Yes, I know. But spare me the details, will ya, Cass?" He tossed the magazine onto his desk, folded his long arms over his broad chest, and peered at her from under sternly lowered brows. "So now I suppose you've got some fool notion of writin' to this fella?"

Cassie averted her gaze and nervously trailed a finger along the smooth edge of her father's massive walnut desk. "You don't think I should?"

"I don't think it's going to matter what I think," her father said with a sniff. "You've probably made up your mind already and, just like your ma, you'll do what you want no matter what I think."

Cassie looked up, suddenly realizing that her father was right. She *had* made up her mind and no amount of talking would change it.

"Dad, I have to contact him. It's only fair."

"Fair to who? I was all for findin' this fella when

you were pregnant, and even when Tyler was just a baby. But it's different now, Cass. Ty's four years old. He's used to us…and we're used to him.'' Jasper's scowl deepened and his arms tightened against his chest. For the second time in her life, Cassie detected fear in her tough ol' daddy's eyes. The first time was when her mother was diagnosed with cancer.

Cassie moved to stand next to her father and laid a gentle hand on his arm. ''You don't think I'm going to allow Adam to take Ty away from here, do you?''

''As a father he'll have rights. He might want joint custody.''

''But there's a much greater chance he won't want anything to do with Tyler,'' Cassie reasoned. She turned away and resumed the idle occupation of tracing invisible designs on her father's desk. ''Besides,'' she began carefully, ''if I write to him and he writes back, and *if* I actually go up there, I might find out he's a jerk. And if that's the case, I'm not even going to tell him about Tyler. I mean, after all, I really didn't get to know him before. We had such a short time together and we weren't exactly exchanging anecdotes about our lives, our families, our aspirations. He might not be the kind of man we want in Tyler's life at all.''

Jasper was silent for such a long time, Cassie was almost afraid to turn and look at him. Because of his strong love for Tyler, Jasper might be reluctant to admit that Adam Baranof had a right to know he was a father, but in the end he'd opt for doing the honorable thing. Would Jasper agree with her that holding off until she knew Adam better was the honorable thing to do?

She turned slowly and faced her father. He was still frowning, but that uncharacteristic frightened look was gone from his eyes. "I don't know if it's the right thing to do or not, Cass. But I don't care. If Ty's gonna have a father in his life, we'd better make damned sure he's a good one. You go ahead and answer that ad and see what happens. Go to Alaska if you want to and keep your secret as long as you need to. You've raised that boy for four years and you've got more rights than this Baranof fella by a long shot. Take it a step at a time, that's what I recommend."

Cassie smiled her relief. "I appreciate your support, Dad."

He patted her on the shoulder and headed for the door. "You've always got it, sweetheart. You know that. Now you'd better get busy and write that letter. If it has to be done, there's no point in putting it off. Use my desk and stationery, if you like."

"Thanks, Dad. I will." Cassie moved to the back of the desk and sat down in her father's cushy leather chair, scooted in and picked up a pen. Then, just before her father was through the door, she called, "Oh, Dad?"

He popped his head in. "Yeah?"

"Do me a favor. Don't tell Brad anything about this till things are more settled, okay?"

He frowned, hesitating. "Okay," he said at last. "But you can do me a favor, too."

"What's that?"

"Be careful this time, will ya?"

Cassie knew her father was referring to more than birth control. What happened with Adam could affect all their lives forever. She hoped her smile conveyed more confidence than she felt as she replied, "Don't worry, Dad. This time I'll look before I leap."

Chapter Two

Wearing his white terry bathrobe and a pair of Nike running shoes, Adam jogged out to the mailbox a half mile down the remote road that led to his cabin, dug out the many envelopes crammed inside and jogged back to the warm house. He dumped the mail on the kitchen table and started sorting it. As had been the case ever since the last issue of *Single Men of Alaska* came out, the stack of letters from women replying to the ad was as high as his orange juice carton. And this was every day. He couldn't wait until he figured out a way to get back at his brother for sending in that stupid ad without his permission.

"I just want you to find a girl and be as happy as I am, bro," his brother had said with that disarming, innocent look of his.

Adam tried to ignore his growing irritation as the stack grew ever higher. He hoped that somewhere at the bottom of this mess he'd find what he was really waiting for—a letter from the National Science Foundation in Washington D.C. telling him that his research grant had been awarded. He was kept busy enough working on the consulting committee for the new aquarium going up in Seward, but he wanted more than anything to continue his research on marine mammal behaviorism and was hoping to start it before summer's end.

When the last envelope turned out to be pink and covered with heart-shaped stickers and lipstick kisses, he had a pretty good idea that it wasn't from a scientist.

Adam swallowed his disappointment, took a sip of coffee from a steaming mug and picked up his letter opener. He'd grudgingly promised his brother to at least read all the letters, even if he had no intention of replying to them. It wasn't that some of the women weren't attractive or didn't sound interesting; it was just that he felt no burning desire to get involved in a relationship right now.

But that was exactly why he'd worded the ad the way he had, his brother had said. Although Alex could vouch for happily-ever-after love as being the best kind ever and worth looking for, none of the women answering the ad would expect more from Adam than friendship.

Adam begged to differ. He opened up the pink envelope first and a photo fell out that was obviously done by one of those boudoir photography studios. The woman was heavily made up, her hair teased to an impossible height, and a pink feather boa encircled her bare shoulders. And talk about cleavage... Her name was Sugar. Sure.

He forced himself to wade through Sugar's flowery scribbles. She wanted candlelight dinners, walks in the rain, single roses on her pillow and...a good stock portfolio. How much did he make as a marine biologist, anyway? Was he interested in moving from Alaska to somewhere more lively...like Vegas?

That one went directly into the trash and was followed by many others. Adam was no longer shocked when he received nude photos or blatant sexual overtures. But he likewise was no longer even remotely interested when the women seemed normal, literate and nice.

By the time he'd made it to the bottom of the pile, his vision was glazed. There was one more letter to wade through, however and, after all, he'd promised. The envelope was a plain white one, which was a welcome sight after so many fuchsias and lavenders. Adam glanced at the return address. This one was from Montana, and the writing was crisp and neat without all those swirls and curlicues it seemed some of the women thought were necessary to convey a proper feeling of romance.

He opened the letter and a photo fell out. He picked it up, glanced at it without much interest, then glanced at it again. It was a young woman, tall, slender, blond, standing by a copper-colored horse. In the background were mountains covered with fir trees and a blue, blue sky. The woman was wearing jeans and a yellow gingham shirt tucked into her belt.

He set down the picture, then picked it up again. There was something about her face...Something so natural and refreshing in the way she'd posed so casually, the wind blowing her straight, shoulder-length hair in a swirl around her head. She was very attractive. Very appealing.

He picked up the letter and read it. Her name was Cassandra Montgomery. Most folks called her Cassie, she wrote. He thought it was a nice name that suited her girl-next-door appearance. She owned a bookstore and coffee bar in a little town called Nye.

Adam tried to remember if he'd stopped in Nye during a trip through Montana a few years ago, but he couldn't recall whether he had or not. There had been so many quaint little towns—especially in the west—he'd lost count of them by the time he'd seen most of the lower forty-nine.

Adam stared at the picture again and tried to imagine her voice. Then he did something he never thought he'd do in a million years. He found some stationery, picked up his pen and wrote back to her.

CASSIE STOOD at the mailbox and held the envelope with trembling fingers. There was no mistaking it. The return address read "Seldovia, Alaska." It was from *him*. Adam. Tyler's father. The only man she'd ever slept with.

"He remembers me," she whispered under her breath as she walked slowly toward the house. Since her father and Sylvie had taken Tyler into town for a matinee, she had the place to herself, and for this she was deeply thankful. She didn't want anyone to see her in this weird state of mixed excitement and dread.

She went to her father's study, which stayed cool even during the hottest summer days, sat down behind his desk and picked up his letter opener. She slit the envelope and removed a neatly folded single sheet of stationery.

She read the short, friendly letter, then read it again. And again. Then she set down the letter and stared at the wall opposite the desk.

"He doesn't remember me," she whispered dismally. But how was it possible that he didn't remember her? And why had he written to her, otherwise? According to his letter, hers was the only letter he'd replied to! Was he lying? But surely she wasn't special enough to pique this man's interest over all other respondents vying for his attention without some remembered history between them. What was going on?

Cassie got up and paced the floor. In the letter he invited her to come to a wedding, his brother's wedding, which was to take place two weeks from Sunday. He said he would send a round-trip, first-class airplane ticket. She could come out on a Thursday, spend the weekend and they'd get to know each other a little bit. At the same time she'd be providing him with a date for the wedding and a safeguard against his Great-Aunt Zelda who would try to set him up with every spare female at the reception afterward.

Cassie appreciated the casual charm and sense of humor evident in his letter writing, but... But why didn't he remember her? Had that evening, which had meant so much to her, meant so little to him?

Two hours later, her father, Sylvie and Tyler came home. Tyler, half asleep, went immediately down for a nap, and Jasper took Cassie by the arm and guided her ahead of him into the study. He closed the door and turned to face her.

"He wrote to you, didn't he?"

"How did you know?"

"You haven't been this pale since you fell off your horse last year and broke your ankle."

Cassie nodded, smiled wanly. "You can read me like a book."

"You're disappointed."

"He didn't remember me. Or if he does, he isn't saying so."

"Why wouldn't he say so?"

"Well, I never let on that *I* remembered *him.*"

Jasper shook his head. "Maybe he's just playing a game he thinks you started. Maybe you should have told him exactly who you are."

"I'm glad I didn't."

"Why?"

"Because, Dad, he doesn't remember me!" Cassie exclaimed, then immediately regretted raising her voice. "Sorry. I'm just not sure what to do now."

"If I were you, I'd still go. If you don't resolve this one way or the other, you'll never stop fretting."

Cassie thought about it, but not for long. "You're right, Dad. I'll write back and tell him to send the ticket. But I want you and Tyler to go with me."

Jasper's eyes widened to the size of silver dollars. "I thought you weren't going to tell him about Tyler until you got to know him a bit? And then only if he impressed you as a good man."

"I still feel that way. I just want you to come with me as far as Anchorage. Adam won't have any idea I didn't come alone. You and Tyler could take in the sights—go fishing for some of that legendary salmon up there—while I find out what I can about this guy. He lives on the Kenai Peninsula, about two hundred miles south of Anchorage. If I tell him about Tyler and he wants to meet him, you guys'll be right there within a half day's road travel. If I don't tell him, or he doesn't want to meet Tyler, well, no big deal. You've said many times that you'd like to visit Alaska. Think of it as a vacation.''

At Jasper's continued doubtful expression, Cassie added cajolingly, ''Besides, Dad, I could use the moral support. Knowing my two favorite guys in the whole world are nearby will really help.''

Although he still looked troubled, Jasper relented and managed a weak smile as he wrapped his arm around Cassie's shoulder. ''Hon, if that's the way you want to do it, I suppose I'll go along with the plan as long it doesn't look like it's about to blow up in your face.''

Cassie nodded gratefully, then added with a furrowed brow, ''What will we tell Brad?''

''That we're taking a vacation. It's partially the truth, but I suppose that means it's partially a lie, too. I hate this, Cassie. Why don't we just tell Brad what's going on?''

''Because I don't think I could deal with Brad's emotions on top of everything else. He's bound to feel threatened.''

Jasper nodded thoughtfully. ''I suppose there's no use worryin' him.''

Cassie agreed wholeheartedly.

BRAD INSISTED on driving them to the airport in Billings, which meant Cassie couldn't relieve any of her tension by talking to her dad about the situation. Instead they were forced to put on a cheerful front as if they were really just going to Alaska for a short vacation.

"My sister and her husband went on a cruise to Alaska a couple of years ago," Brad commented conversationally as they sped along the interstate. "She couldn't quit talking about it for weeks after. She said Prince William Sound was the most beautiful place she'd ever seen."

Cassie turned to look at Brad, at his strong tanned hands on the steering wheel, at his clean, honest profile below a thatch of blond hair, the sun-wrinkles around his blue eyes. She was almost sure he suspected something was going on that he wasn't included in, but he was being polite and patient as usual. Sometimes Cassie wished he'd be just a little demanding and difficult. Maybe if he had been, they'd be married by now and she'd have one thing less to worry about on this trip.

Cassie glanced into the back seat where her father and Tyler were reading a book together. Her gaze locked with her father's for a moment and she knew they were sharing the same concerns.

"Will you see Prince William Sound?" Brad asked her, turning his head to look at her.

"I'm not sure," Cassie answered with a smile. "Our itinerary isn't exactly worked out yet."

Brad nodded, looked at her doubtfully for a minute, then turned his gaze back to the road without saying another word.

Yep, thought Cassie. *He knows something's up.*

AFTER SEEMING to almost skim the peaks of the Chugach Mountains east of the city, the plane descended quickly to land at Anchorage International Airport at five o'clock Thursday afternoon. For a minute, Cassie thought they were going to land in Cook Inlet itself, but soon realized that the gray water adjacent to the regular landing strips of the airport was Lake Hood, which the pilot had mentioned over the intercom as being the busiest seaplane base in the world. It was fascinating to look down on hundreds of small, colorful planes docked in the water.

Since Adam had arranged to meet her at the gate, Cassie said goodbye to her father and Tyler in the airplane, then waited for them to get off and far enough away before she disembarked. Tyler was happy to go with his granddad, and he was assured that his mommy would see him in a couple of days. He was reminded of when she went away every once in awhile to booksellers' conventions. He knew she'd always come back and, in the meantime, he and his granddad could go fishing. He was enthralled with the possibility of catching a fish bigger than he was.

As Cassie walked through the covered ramp, clutching her purse and the two carry-ons which held everything she'd brought for the trip, she hoped the long flight hadn't made her look like death warmed over. You couldn't tell anything by those tiny mirrors they had in the in-flight rest rooms, but she had made sure her hair was neatly combed, her bangs smooth and her lipstick fresh.

As for her clothes, the only reasonable choice for

surviving a long flight with a small boy was to wear jeans and a casual wrinkle-proof knit top—navy blue, so stains wouldn't show as much. And, as she knew it got cool in the evenings in Alaska even in summer, she'd tied a blue-and-white-patterned sweater around her shoulders to wear later.

The last one off the plane, she emerged from the ramp and stopped cold, looking around cautiously. She suddenly realized that she was absolutely petrified. But it was too late to turn tail and run because there he was. *Adam.* He was headed straight for her, as big as life, all smiles and twice as handsome as she remembered. He wore jeans and a crew-neck sweater that was the exact shade of sky-blue as his eyes.

Memories of that night came flooding back.

The feel of his lips, the taste of him.

His strong arms as he held her close…

Cassie's heart was beating so hard and fast she had a sudden unreasonable fear that Adam might actually be able to see its frantic rhythm under the thin fabric of her blouse.

"Hey, I was beginning to think you'd chickened out," he teased, standing in front of her with his hands propped casually on his lean hips.

He sounded exactly the way she remembered. "I…I almost did," Cassie admitted, smiling shyly.

He stared at her for a few seconds, his gaze studying her features with an intensity that made Cassie hope he was remembering, too.

"Your voice…" he began.

"Yes?" Cassie prompted eagerly.

He smiled again. "It's just like I imagined it

would be. That's what really made me write to you, Cassie. After seeing your picture, I had to find out how your voice sounded."

Cassie hid her profound disappointment and glibly replied, "So if I sounded like Olive Oyl you'd have put me on the next plane back to Montana, I suppose?"

He laughed and reached out to take her luggage. In the process, their hands brushed and a thrill went up Cassie's arm like a shock of electricity. Startled, she didn't dare look at him and instead stared at the floor. She couldn't believe the attraction could be so immediate—and stronger than ever!

"We only have a short way to walk," he said, his voice calm, his manner collected as he took her elbow and guided her toward the open terminal. The light touch of his fingers against her skin gave her goose bumps.

"Are you cold?" he asked suddenly.

Cassie gave herself a stern mental lecture. She had to pull herself together. She was ashamed to be so easily attracted to this man. Especially since he didn't seem to be affected by her in the same way.

She forced a smile. "Maybe a little. The plane was hot and it's really open in here."

"Alaska is famous for its wide-open spaces. I think you're going to like your visit. This is incredible country. But then Montana's pretty incredible, too."

Cassie searched his face. "Have you been there?"

"Yes. But it was several years ago and I have to admit I don't remember a lot about it. You'll have

to refresh my memory. Now, why don't we stop for
a minute so you can put on your sweater?''

While Adam solicitously helped her on with her
sweater, Cassie fumed. *Oh, I'd like to refresh your
memory, all right. How about with a cricket mallet
to the head?*

"There, is that better?"

Cassie nodded and smiled, outwardly all sweetness and light, inwardly getting more frustrated by
the minute. How could he have forgotten her so
completely? Surely, though, once they'd talked for
four hours during the trip to Seldovia, he'd start to
remember. And, if he didn't, it would serve him
right if she just surprised him with the news suddenly—kind of like a splash of cold water to the
face. *Something* was needed to wake this guy up!

But Cassie soon found out that it wasn't going to
take four hours to get to their destination. Adam
walked her through the terminal to a shuttle, which
quickly transported them to Lake Hood.

"We're going in a floatplane?" she squeaked as
she peered through the shuttle window.

Adam chuckled, then climbed out and turned to
face her. "It's a fast way to get around and a great
way to get your first glimpse of the land, Cassie.
Are you nervous?"

"Are you the pilot?"

"Yes. But don't worry. I've been flying since I
was sixteen. Trust me?"

He held out his hand and she looked at it for a
minute, traitorous memories recalling the feel of his
caresses, then placed her hand in his. "Sure, I trust

you,'' she said flippantly, although she'd never been in a plane smaller than a jet in her life.

"You'll love it," he assured her.

And she did, right from the minute she climbed aboard the compact blue-and-white plane and took off in an exhilarating spray of water.

"It's a de Havilland DHC2 Beaver, but I call her *Tashya.*"

Thinking of "Bogie," Cassie turned to him. "You like nicknames?"

"If they apply. I named this little beauty after my grandmother, Natashya Nikolski Baranof. Small and beautiful, almost delicate-looking, but strong and reliable and full of spunk."

Cassie liked the "reliable" part, because it seemed as though they were barely airborne when Anchorage abruptly ended and a vast wilderness began! There were mountains, meadows, rivers and lakes. Oh, so many lakes! Despite her tumbled emotions, she couldn't help but be delightfully distracted by the incredible scenery she was flying over.

"What's that? It looks like a field of snow."

"It's arctic cotton. And that meadow over there at the base of the mountain is full of red fireweed and purple lupine."

"Beautiful. And what about that mass of brown. I think it's moving!"

"It's a herd of caribou. I doubt you'll ever see as many animals anywhere as you'll see here in Alaska. Look, there's a flock of migrating cranes."

Cassie looked and looked and asked a million questions—even forgetting in the excitement of the moment that she was peeved at the pilot. But, really, hitting a man with the news that he was a father as the result of a one-night stand he didn't even remember while he piloted a plane over the rugged terrain of Alaska did not seem the wisest move, anyway. There'd be a right time for telling him later, and meanwhile she could try to get to know something more about the man who'd fathered her son.

Adam proved to be a font of information, a definite lover of the land. "Have you always lived in Alaska?" she asked him.

"Yes. In fact, my roots go back to the eighteenth century. My Russian ancestors settled on Kodiak Island and now they're all over the state."

"What about your immediate family?"

"My immediate family is settled mostly around Cook Inlet in small towns like Homer and Seldovia. In fact, my father runs a charter boat business out of Homer. You know, tours for fishing, hunting and sight-seeing. My mother used to work in Dad's business, but she stays at home now and thoroughly enjoys that."

"What about your brother?"

Adam smiled at her as if surprised and flattered by her curiosity. "My brother is a marine geologist, rather than a biologist like me. He works for the oil companies by helping them locate sites on the seafloor to drill for petroleum and natural gas. He's a lot more practical than I am."

Cassie couldn't resist it. "Is that why he's getting married and you're not?"

Adam chuckled and eyed her warily. "I've never considered marriage a practical goal. I just figured two people met and fell in love, realized they wanted to stay together forever, then got married as the next natural step.''

Cassie couldn't argue with that. In fact, he hadn't said anything that she could argue with. He seemed intelligent, polite, friendly and a perfect gentleman. So far, there had been absolutely nothing in his conversation or manners that could remotely justify not telling him about Tyler...except for the fact that he didn't seem to have the vaguest memory of having slept with the mother of his son! But maybe, although it was a crushing blow to her pride, Cassie shouldn't hold his faulty memory against him. After all, what did that have to do with Tyler?

They were following the shoreline of Cook Inlet now, on the east side of Kenai Peninsula where the mountains gave way to dense forests that rolled down to narrow beaches. In the space of about an hour, during which they continued to chat about a wide variety of things—excluding one-night stands and unplanned pregnancies—they touched down in the deep-blue waters of Kachemac Bay, an arm of the inlet. They taxied to a wooden dock, pulling abreast a tied-up motorboat. From the dock, rustic-looking stairs climbed the thickly forested hillside and disappeared into the shrubbery.

''This looks like a beautiful place,'' Cassie said as she peered through the front window of the plane. ''But sort of remote.''

''That's the way I like it,'' Adam said, as he turned dials and flicked switches on the control board. When he was finished, he gave her a devilish smile. ''It's even more remote than you think, Cassie. The only way to get out of Seldovia is by ferry or plane, so even if you decide this blind date is a bummer, you're at my mercy till you can figure out the ferry schedule or learn to fly. Although, sometimes my brother Alex drops by. He lives in Seldovia proper, near the ferry dock. You could always plead your case to him.''

Cassie laughed nervously at his teasing, not so much worried about being at *his* mercy as she was at being at the mercy of her own traitorous attraction to this Alaskan hunk.

''Homer—you know, where my folks live—is on the other side of the bay,'' Adam told her when they stood on the dock and Cassie stared in awe in a different direction across the inlet at huge, snow-capped peaks that rose from sea level, and at what seemed like a river of blue ice.

''That's Grewingk Glacier,'' Adam informed her without waiting for the question that hovered on Cassie's lips. ''I'm glad it's clear today, so you can see it. Pretty amazing, huh?''

Cassie could only nod. She was trying to withstand the double whammy of being thrilled simultaneously by the man at her side and the breathtaking scenery that surrounded her.

''Let's get you up to the house,'' he said, after allowing her a couple more minutes of awed staring. ''We'll have plenty of time to sightsee, and there's a lot I want to show you. Come on, Cass.''

Cassie preceded Adam up the stairs toward a large wood-frame cabin set on rock pilings. As she ascended, she saw and heard birds and insects and small animals grubbing through the undergrowth. The place pulsed with life.

At the top of the stairs where the land leveled off, Cassie saw a green Jeep Cherokee parked on a gravel driveway next to the cabin. They went inside the cabin, which, if not palatial was definitely substantial in size, quite open and airy, and with all the modern amenities.

After a quick tour of the house—which, as one might expect in a bachelor pad, was rather sparsely furnished and decorated—Adam surprised her by taking her outside again and walking her to another, much smaller cabin just a few yards away. It was connected to the main house by a wooden walkway that bypassed a large, screened-in hot tub nestled among spruce and birch trees.

"I guess you could call this the guest house for want of a better term," he said when she looked to him for an explanation. "It was kind of a bonus when I bought the place. I don't use it much, but my parents sometimes send family and out-of-town guests over here when they run out of room at their place. Since we don't know each other that well yet, I thought you'd be more comfortable out here."

Cassie nodded mutely and followed him inside. Remembering how quickly they had gotten chummy at their first meeting, she had been prepared to ask for her own separate bedroom. But he was actually putting her in a separate *house!* Either he'd become more reserved over the past five years, or she just didn't turn him on anymore. Confused, Cassie wasn't sure which explanation she preferred.

Adam showed her through the cozy cabin, then moved to the door, saying, "Feel free to use the hot tub. It's a great way to loosen up after a long flight.

Dinner'll be ready at eight-thirty.'' He grinned. "I'm a pretty good cook, so I hope you're hungry."

"Oh, I am," Cassie lied. She didn't think she could swallow a bite. There was too much left unsaid, too much tension. She was dying to blurt out the truth, to tell him that he had a son that looked exactly like him, right down to the cleft in his chin. And to demand to know why the hell he didn't have the slightest memory of having slept with the mother of their adorable child!

Adam smiled again, oblivious to her frustration. "Good. Don't bother knocking when you come up to the main house. Just walk in. See you later."

"Yeah. See you later," she echoed.

As soon as Adam shut the door behind him, Cassie sank onto the bed, physically and emotionally exhausted. She realized there was no way she was going to be able to keep up this charade much longer. And maybe there was no reason to.

Maybe Adam had slept around a lot five years ago and that's why he didn't remember her, but appearances seemed to indicate that he no longer practiced that same life-style. Otherwise, wouldn't he have at least put her under the same roof so it would be easier to get her into his bed?

Cassie sighed and made a resolution. She was done with this waiting game. At dinner—maybe even *before* dinner—she was going to tell him everything.

ADAM FOUND himself whistling as he prepared trout almandine, a spinach salad and crusty rolls, then set the table with the good dishes his mother had given him as a housewarming gift three years ago which he had never used. He even picked some yellow arctic poppies from the yard and plopped them in a vase he found collecting dust in the back of his cupboard, then lit a couple of fat emergency candles he kept around in case the electric generator broke down and arranged them near the flowers. Maybe they weren't elegant tapers, but their flickering flames still set a sort of mood.

Adam couldn't believe he was so intrigued by this woman, so immediately attracted to her, so eager to make a good impression. It wasn't in his nature to be impetuous, but he already knew without a doubt that he wanted to get to know as much as he could about Cassandra Montgomery.

He leaned against the counter as the fish sizzled in the pan and thought about her. She was lovely and natural. Despite her many questions, there was a reticence about her, a sort of "mystery." But this was a welcome change from all the women who came on like gangbusters on the first date.

He was actually thinking of calling his brother to thank him for putting that stupid ad in the magazine! But there was no time. Cassie would walk through that door any minute and he had no intention of being on the phone. Tomorrow things would start getting hectic, beginning with a morning trip into Kenai for a final fitting of his tux. Saturday was the rehearsal, Sunday was the wedding, and Monday she was scheduled to fly home. Suddenly four days just seemed like far too little time to get to know this lovely woman. But maybe, if things went well, he could convince her to stay longer.

"Knock, knock?"

He turned and saw her standing just inside the door. He liked what he saw. She had changed into a pair of beige linen slacks and a long-sleeved, silky-looking white blouse. Her hair fell in a shiny blunt cut to her shoulders and her bangs were brushed to the side. She wore a minimum of makeup and pale freckles dotted her small, straight nose. She managed to look natural and elegant at the same time.

"Come in, Cassie." He walked up to her and impetuously took her hands, gazing into her gray eyes until she blushed and turned away. "You look great."

She pulled her hands away and walked past him into the room, stopped at the table, then turned to face him. "This is nice." She made a sweeping gesture of the neatly set table. "You must do a lot of entertaining."

"Hardly," he said with a rueful smile. "I cleaned the place just for you, and this is the first time those dishes have seen the light of day. I usually eat off paper plates."

She looked at him doubtfully as if she didn't believe him. "I'm sure you don't serve wonderful dishes like trout almandine—that *is* what I'm smelling, isn't it?—on disposable dinnerware to your guests."

Adam walked back to the stove to tend to dinner and spoke to her over the counter that separated the kitchen from the dining area. "No, I don't. I don't because I hardly ever have guests. In fact, I've been so wrapped up in my work lately, the last time I had a date was—" he paused and mentally ticked off the time "—two months ago, to be precise. And I didn't bring her here because I couldn't be bothered to clean up the place. Bachelors will be bachelors, you know. We're very predictable."

She nodded, her smooth brow furrowing slightly. "Oh, I wouldn't say that. At least *you're* not."

Adam didn't know what to reply, but it appeared that he wasn't expected to. Cassie immediately turned away and began to slowly pace the living room floor, apparently deep in thought.

Now Adam frowned. It didn't seem to him to be a good sign for your date to be in a contemplative funk not five minutes into the evening. He turned off the stove and walked around the counter to stand by the table with his arms crossed over his chest, watching her.

When she appeared not to even notice his presence, he finally asked, "Is something the matter, Cassie? You seem very preoccupied."

She turned abruptly, a strange sort of urgent expression in her eyes. "Something *is* the matter, Adam."

He took two steps forward. She took two steps back and began to wring her hands. "What is it?" he demanded, starting to worry. All sorts of possibilities were going through his head. Hell, he hoped she wasn't going to tell him she was married!

"There's something I have to tell you."

He sighed. Such a beginning did not sound promising. "Go ahead."

Her head bobbed nervously. She gave a wan smile and wrung her hands a little more. "It's about when you were in Montana before—"

"Yes?" he prompted.

"You and I..." She paused again, blushing.

Now he was really confused. "You and I what?"

"You and I—"

But Cassie had no chance to finish her confession, or revelation or whatever it was she was trying to say, because just then the door swung open and a man breezed in.

"Hey, bro," Adam began, then caught sight of Cassie just as she caught sight of his brother. Her eyes widened and her lips parted on a startled gasp. That's when Adam realized he hadn't told Cassie that he and his brother were—

"Twins," Cassie said in a shaky voice. "Oh, my God. You're *twins*."

Chapter Three

Cassie grabbed the back of one of the dining room chairs for support. She felt faint. Her insides were topsy-turvy. She couldn't believe she was looking at two men who were absolutely identical in appearance, from handsome head to toe, both of whom—no, *either* of whom—could be the father of her child! But since Adam didn't seem to remember her, maybe it was his brother who was actually Tyler's father. There was only one way to find out.

"Cassie, you don't look too well," she heard Adam say as he laid a hand on her shoulder and peered worriedly into her face. "Maybe you should sit down."

"I don't want to sit down. I want to ask your brother a question."

Looking perplexed, Adam gazed back and forth between his brother and Cassie. Alex had no expression on his face whatsoever. He simply stared, as if in a trance. "You want to ask Alex a question? But you two don't even know each other." He paused, then his brows lowered. He turned back to his brother. "Or do you?"

"That's a good question. *Do* we know each other, Alex?" Cassie quickly echoed, hating the note of desperation that had crept into her voice. But now that she'd started, she couldn't stop. She wanted an end to this uncertainty. "Are you the man I met five years ago at the Fourth of July fair in Nye, Montana, whom I then spent the night with at the Tuddenhams' bed-and-breakfast?"

Cassie heard Adam gasp, but her gaze was fixed on Alex, willing him to speak, to react in some way. When he continued to appear stunned and confused, she turned back to Adam, tears beginning to sting the back of her eyelids. "Or is it you, Adam, and you just don't remember me?"

Now both men appeared stupefied. "Don't just stand there like a couple of idiots!" Cassie exclaimed, beyond exasperation. "One of you *must* remember me, because one of you happens to be the father of my four-year-old son! He looks exactly like you—exactly like *both* of you! Right down to that damned cleft in your chins!"

In almost perfect unison, Adam and Alex both fumbled for chairs and sat down.

"I'm not telling you this because I want money from you," Cassie hurriedly explained. "I don't want child support for Tyler. We're perfectly fine the way we are. He's got plenty of male influence in his life, too, and doesn't necessarily need a father. I just thought you should know about him, that's all. And, someday when he asks, I want to be able to tell my son who his father is. That's why I answered Adam's ad. That's why I came up here. I saw the face of Tyler's father in that magazine, staring back at me after five years, and it was the only way I knew him. Now what I want is a name. Is it Adam or is it Alex?''

Adam and Alex seemed to be in states of shock because neither of them said anything. It was either that or...

Cassie dropped her head into her hands. "Oh, my God. *Neither* of you remembers me, do you? Adam, where's your bathroom? I think I'm going to be sick.''

This announcement finally stirred Adam to action. He hurried to his feet, caught her arm and guided her to a bathroom that seemed miles away by the time Cassie got there. She sagged down onto the edge of the tub and gratefully received the washcloth Adam quickly dampened and handed to her.

"Are you really going to be sick?" he inquired gently.

"I don't know," Cassie answered dully. "But if I do get sick, I don't want you here to see it. With my luck, you'd remember the sight of me puking my guts out even if you can't remember making love to me all night long.''

"Cassie, I—"

"Go away. Shut the door and go away. I need some time.''

Cassie waited until he left, then she turned on the tap, redampened the washcloth with steamy-hot water, bent her head and gratefully pressed the washcloth to the back of her neck. She kept the tap running to drown out the sound just in case she started crying.

All the tension, all the doubt of the past couple

of weeks had come to a head…and *still* nothing was resolved! Damn it, she almost wanted to cry—maybe it would make her feel better—but a stubborn part of her refused to. She'd have her little time out, then she'd march out there again for another dose of necessary humiliation. By sorting out travel agendas of five years ago, surely they'd be able to figure out which of the forgetful Baranof twins was Tyler's father.

WHEN ADAM RETURNED to the dining room, Alex was still seated in the chair, looking dazed. Adam crossed his arms and stood over him, his knees locked, his legs slightly spread in an almost military stance. He stared down at his brother until Alex raised his head to meet his stern gaze.

"Is she going to be all right?"

"That depends. *Do* you remember her, Alex?"

Alex sighed. "Of course I do." Wearily, he ran a hand through his hair. "I recognized her immediately. It was such a shock, for a minute or two I couldn't even breathe." Then in a quieter, softer tone, he continued, "It would be impossible to forget that night."

Alex felt a sharp stab of jealousy which he tried to squelch. This was a serious matter that needed to be discussed calmly and rationally, without emotional distractions.

"Was it just one night?"

"Yes. We had a date for lunch the next day, but I left town before she came by."

Adam fought the urge to whack his brother upside the head. "That was a crummy thing to do."

"I didn't mean to do it. I got a call from Mom. It was when Dad got that concussion and he was in critical care. We all rushed to his bedside, remember?"

Adam nodded, then asked gruffly, "Didn't you two even exchange names?"

"She told me her name, but I only told her my frat nickname."

Adam grimaced. "Bogie?"

"Yeah."

"And she was satisfied with that?"

Alex shrugged tiredly. "I guess so. Hell, I was just having fun, Adam. I even registered under Mr. Bogart. I did that all the time, back then. I was going to tell her my real name the next day." He looked earnestly at Adam. "I know I've done a lot of stupid, irresponsible things in my life, bro, but I certainly never intended to get Cassie in trouble then abandon her."

Adam's anger subsided...a little. Anyway, he had an inkling that his anger was partially based on the fact that his brother had found Cassie first...and had left with her such a permanent reminder of himself.

"What are you going to do about the child?"

"The child." Alex shuddered. "I can't believe this. How can this be happening little more than forty-eight hours before my wedding? When Kelly finds out I have an illegitimate son, she'll... she'll—" He shook his head woefully. "Hell, I don't have a clue what she'll do, but it'll definitely put a damper on what's supposed to be the most wonderful day of her life. As for her parents...I've

got a pretty good idea how *they'll* react to the news.''

Adam knew exactly what Alex meant. Alex's intended in-laws were quite a bit older than their own parents and had had Kelly, the youngest of their seven children, late in life. They were old-fashioned and very protective. When they'd found out that Kelly had been living with Alex since their engagement three months before, Mrs. Armstrong had cried and Mr. Armstrong was so angry he almost refused to fly out from their home in Florida for the wedding. Kelly mollified him by moving into her own apartment until she and Alex were actually married.

Adam had met Mr. and Mrs. Armstrong at a family dinner the day before and, while Mr. Armstrong was polite and pleasant, he clearly adored his daughter and did not seem to be the sort of man who could easily overlook the sudden appearance of a woman from Alex's past claiming a child as the result of a one-night stand.

Mr. Armstrong strongly disapproved of alcoholic beverages, too, not just for himself but for the whole world, and was opposed to serving it at the wedding reception. Kelly gave in to him on this, just as she had on her living arrangements, and champagne was omitted from the menu.

Adam felt that people had a right to make their own choices about whether or not to drink alcoholic beverages, and felt it was rather selfish of Mr. Armstrong to try to force his own personal code of behavior not just on his adult daughter but on everyone else. Unfortunately, if Mr. Armstrong was that opinionated about champagne consumption, he would probably have even stronger opinions about one-night stands and accidental babies. Adam was beginning to feel some reluctant sympathy for Alex.

"I don't suppose there's any chance Cassie's lying," Adam suggested tentatively. The two brothers locked gazes and simultaneously shook heads. "No, I didn't think so, either," Adam muttered. He hardly knew her, but he instinctively realized Cassie was probably too honest for her own good. Besides, all she had to do was produce a picture of Tyler, and if he looked as much like Alex as she said, who could dispute that kind of evidence?

"She was a virgin," Alex suddenly revealed.

Adam clenched his jaw. That was more information than he wanted. "I repeat, Alex, what are you going to do about the child?"

With much effort, Alex pulled himself to his feet and began to trudge about the room, his hands stuffed in the back pockets of his jeans. "Hell, I don't know! What am I supposed to do?"

"By Cassie's account, nothing. She doesn't seem to care whether you're part of the child's life or not. She says she doesn't want money, or your influence as a parent. I think she just wanted to end the embarrassment of not knowing the name of her child's father." Adam paused, then asked, "Don't you have *any* interest in the boy, Alex?"

"Not really," Alex admitted a little sheepishly. "Right now all I can think about is Kelly and the life we've got planned, and how all that's in jeopardy now! You know how long I've waited for a woman like Kelly, Adam. I can't stand the thought that I might lose her."

Alex moved to the window and looked out over the heavily wooded hill behind the cabin. Adam watched the glum profile of his younger brother— by exactly three minutes—and his sympathy grew. It was true, Alex had waited a long time for a woman like Kelly.

Well, perhaps *waiting* wasn't the right word to describe Alex's activities before he met Kelly. Charm incarnate, Alex had always attracted more women than he knew what to do with. As a scientist and a scholar, he was exemplary. As a date or a lover, he was irresponsible and fickle. That is, until steady, levelheaded, strong-minded—except when up against her parents—lovely Kelly Armstrong came along. Paradoxically, being head-over-heels in love with her had grounded him for the first time in his life.

They were both geologists, both career-minded, and had jobs lined up in Florida, where they planned to move after the honeymoon. Kelly was just what Alex needed, and her presence had considerably lessened Adam's struggles with his younger twin, as well. Lord knew he'd helped his brother get through the hassles of countless soured relationships over the years, and it was a relief to see Alex finally happy and committed. It would be a terrible shame to have it all blow up in his face because of something that happened five years ago.

"Adam?"

"Hmm?" Adam roused himself from thought and was surprised to find his brother looking at him with something like hope on his face.

"I think I've got a solution to this problem.

Something that will satisfy Cassie and save my marriage, too.'' He spoke in a whisper now, darting a look toward the hallway from which Cassie might emerge at any moment.

Adam frowned suspiciously. ''What are you talking about, Alex?''

Alex moved closer, his tone urgent and excited. ''Just tell Cassie that *you're* Tyler's father! That it was *you* who slept with her five years ago!''

Adam instinctively recoiled from such an idea. ''What? You're crazy, Alex! Number one, it wouldn't be fair to lie about something as important as a child's paternity. Number two, she wouldn't believe me. I haven't shown a single sign of having recognized her since she arrived.''

Alex grabbed Adam's shoulder in a clench so tight it hurt. ''Number one, you're the kid's uncle, aren't you? You look just like his real father, don't you? You're a Baranof. How much closer to the real thing could she get? And, number two, just tell her that you were drunk that night, or...or something. That *now* you remember her. That she'd seemed familiar all along, but it took the jolt of her news to jog your memory.''

''I would never have forgotten sleeping with Cassie, drunk or sober,'' Adam stately grimly. ''*You* didn't forget.''

''No, but she doesn't know that. She went into the bathroom not knowing which of us was the father, thinking that whoever it was had forgotten the whole...er...incident. Hell, she'll be relieved to find out it's you and not me! She'd probably be the last person to want to mess up anyone's wedding.''

Adam shook his head. "There has to be another solution. What if Cassie agreed to keep quiet about Tyler's paternity till after the honeymoon? You could break it to your fiancée then without her father around to fan the fire. Or tell Kelly now, just keep it from her parents. She'd probably understand."

"Would she? I don't know. She's caved in to her parents more than once. She moved out on me when her father voiced his disapproval of our living arrangements, remember? And why should *I* take the risk?"

Alex cocked a brow. "Because *you're* the father?"

"But *you* don't have a fiancée to worry about! Besides, I'll bet Cassie would be hurt if we tried to hush up the whole thing. It would be best for everyone if you just claimed paternity. Cassie'll go home happy and I'll go on my honeymoon happy."

Adam wanted to ask, *but what about me?* There was nothing about this situation making *him* happy. Cassie may have only answered Adam's ad because she thought he was Alex, but he had written to her because of an immediate and unexpectedly powerful attraction to her. Meeting her in person had only intensified that attraction. It seemed grossly unfair that she was suddenly off-limits to him because of a complicated history with his brother. His brother…who probably wished he'd never set eyes on Cassie in his life.

And she was definitely off-limits. Without honesty between them, to try to initiate an intimate relationship would be brutally unfair. Considering his attraction to her, if he went along with Alex's idea and she stuck around for the wedding as planned, the next three days could be a living hell.

But maybe he deserved a little bit of hell for such a great big lie...if he agreed to tell it.

And what about Cassie and what *she* deserved? Did she deserve the truth, which would almost certainly put many lives in upheaval? Or did she deserve a lie that would probably—excluding himself—smooth the way for them all?

Tyler wouldn't suffer. He was far away in Montana and would never have to meet either him or Alex. Tyler's life would go blissfully on and when the day came when he asked his mother about his real father, he'd find out it was a man in Alaska named Baranof. Did the first name matter?

Why *not* take the path of least resistance? Adam rationalized. Alex's self-interest notwithstanding, maybe he was right. Maybe it was the best course to take, after all.

"I'm back."

Adam's head jerked up to find Cassie standing just inside the room. He expected to see her eyes pink from crying, but they weren't. She was very pale, but she stood straight and tall, with her chin up. *Stoic.* He wished he could take her into his arms to caress and comfort her until the color crept back into her cheeks and that grim look about her soft mouth disappeared.

"Are you okay?"

She nodded, tried to smile. "Yes, I'm much better now. It was just a shock, you know, seeing you both together like that. I had no idea..." She gave an uncertain chuckle. "It shot my theory all to heck about who Tyler's father absolutely had to be. Now there are two possibilities.'' She looked from Adam to Alex, who was standing with his back to the room, facing the window again, then back to Adam. ''Has...has either of you remembered...anything?''

Alex looked over his shoulder at Adam, his eyes pleading, urging. Cassie's expression was wrenchingly hopeful. Adam had never felt more torn in his life. While his conscience screamed foul, his emotions were nevertheless winning the battle.

Finally, with a sigh of surrender, he said, ''Yes, Cassie. I remember. I remember that night with you.''

Adam was immediately rewarded for his lie. Cassie's eyes lost their bleakness, her shoulders their rigidity, her mouth its grim pucker. And, in the background, Alex's head dropped in an almost prayerful pose of profound relief.

''Then...then you're Tyler's father,'' Cassie said, as if needing to reassure herself by stating the obvious.

Adam's gaze darted to Alex, then away. It was hard to look at his brother and lie about the father thing. ''Yes. Yes, I guess I am.''

Cassie nodded slowly. ''Then I guess we have some things to talk about.''

''That's my cue to leave,'' Alex spoke up, turning and walking briskly past them to the door. With his hand on the knob, he glanced back at them, a smile plastered on his face, but Adam detected behind the politeness the look of a hunted man who had just escaped a death trap. ''You guys do have a lot to talk about. I'll see you tomorrow in Kenai for the tux fitting. Cassie, you can meet Kelly then. You'll love her.''

Cassie nodded absently, her eyes still fixed on Adam.

Alex paused, then added nervously, "Right, Adam?"

Adam looked at his brother, his expression carefully neutral. He already had a sinking feeling in his stomach that what he'd just done was terribly wrong. But the die was cast. "Right, Alex. See you tomorrow.''

ALEX WAS GONE and Cassie was alone with Adam. Now that the truth was out, she felt horribly self-conscious. She had been prepared to feel awkward at this point, but the surprising arrival of Adam's twin had almost turned the drama of the situation into *melo*drama.

"I feel like I'm living in a soap opera," Cassie confessed, hoping to lighten the mood.

"All the key elements are present," Adam agreed with a grim, rueful smile. "Amnesia, babies out of the blue, evil twin."

"*Evil* twin?" Cassie teased gamely. "Which one?"

Adam looked away and shrugged. "Are you hungry, Cassie? Dinner's still edible.''

"I don't think I can eat a bite till we've cleared some things up," she admitted.

He nodded and pulled out a chair for her. "Okay. Sit down. We'll talk, then eat."

She sat down, scooted her chair near the table, then rested her clasped hands in front of her. Adam sat opposite her, but he leaned back, his arms crossed high over his chest. Cassie thought the pose rather standoffish and defensive and it prompted her first question.

"You're not at all happy about this news, are you?"

His lips twitched. "I would have thought the first thing you'd want to know is why I didn't remember you right away."

"That *is* a good question. Another good question is, why do you remember me now?"

Adam's blue eyes narrowed slightly as his gaze trailed over her features. She felt warmth creep up her neck. "Your face immediately caught my attention, Cassie. Your face out of hundreds of faces on hundreds of photos."

"I suppose that *does* mean you remembered me, whether you knew it or not, because otherwise you would never have written to me out of all those respondents to your ad. It would just be too weird. Too coincidental...or fated."

He blinked, smiled tightly. "Right. Too coincidental, too fated."

"Then, when I blurted out the bare facts, I can see you finally putting two and two together. But, honestly, I can't understand you forgetting so *completely* until then."

"The details are fuzzy, Cassie, because...because I was drunk that night."

Cassie stared. The confession seemed to have been wrenched out of him. "You're kidding. You certainly didn't act drunk. You were very... well...*coordinated*." If he was so skillful and romantic when he was drunk, what was he like sober? She didn't dare think about it.

"You'd be surprised how drunk a man can be and still…er…perform normally," he informed her with another grim smile.

She may never have been with another man, but Cassie knew Adam had to be above average in the lovemaking department. She just knew it.

She noticed a muscle ticking in his jaw. Had she made him angry?

"You don't seem to care for this line of questioning," she suggested.

"I feel stupid about remembering so little." He uncrossed his arms, crossed a long leg ankle to knee and absently tapped the sole of his shoe with a forefinger. His movements and mannerisms were still graceful, still fascinating to watch. "Aren't you insulted?"

Cassie recalled her wandering thoughts. "Yes, I suppose I am…a little. Especially since I remember so *much*."

Adam grunted. There was a beat of uncomfortable silence, then he said, "I know one detail that's rather significant."

"What is it?"

"It was your first time."

Cassie blushed again and stared at her clasped hands. After such an unpromising beginning, he was certainly remembering more than she expected him to.

"I suppose you remember that because I was a klutz that night. Because I didn't know what I was doing till…till you showed me. But it all seemed so natural, and I got the impression that you enjoyed yourself as much…as much as I did.''

When he didn't immediately answer, Cassie braved a glance at him. The muscle in his jaw was ticking more frantically than ever. ''I've put you on the spot, haven't I? I'm sorry. I don't know why I even brought up any of this. Anyway, how can you reassure me about something you barely remember?''

Adam stared at Cassie's flushed, embarrassed face. He'd never felt so frustrated in his life. While he wanted more than anything to reassure her about that night, he'd be treading through uncharted territory to do so. He could only guess how things had gone that night, only suppose they'd gone well. By her and Alex's reactions to every mention of it, perhaps *extremely* well. Besides, if Cassie had enjoyed herself so much, it stood to reason that Alex couldn't have helped but enjoy himself, too. *Damn* him.

Adam gazed into her clear-as-crystal eyes just before Cassie ducked her head shyly and looked down. He decided that there probably wasn't a man on earth who could resist such a woman's charms. Least of all his three-minutes-younger brother. And since he'd already told Cassie an enormous lie to ease the way to happiness for that brother, he shouldn't feel the least compunction about telling smaller lies that would make her happy, too.

''You weren't a klutz, Cassie.''

Up flew her downcast eyes. ''I wasn't?''

''Far from it. As you said yourself, it…it was all very natural. Very lovely. I enjoyed myself very much and I was sorry I couldn't meet you for lunch the next day. I got a phone call, you see. My father had a fall and my mother called to—''

"Ah." Her eyes lit up, her lips curved in a tentative smile. "So it *was* an emergency. You didn't stand me up?"

He smiled back and answered honestly. "A man would be a damned fool to break a date with you for any reason short of a major emergency." Impulsively he reached across the table and took her hands. "I'm sorry that I... What I mean is, I'm just sorry you had to go through so much alone, with the baby and all."

She squeezed his hands and her smile broadened, its sweetness sending an unwilling surge of emotion through him. "There's nothing to feel sorry about when it comes to Tyler. I loved him from the moment he was conceived. I loved being pregnant and I've loved being his mother."

Adam nodded doubtfully. "Yes, but there must have been difficulties—"

"Oh, there were," she answered with a wry chuckle. "Not the least of which was my father, who wanted to tar and feather you."

Adam released her hands and sat back. "That's understandable," he murmured.

"But he doesn't want to do that anymore, because he's as crazy about Tyler as I am."

Adam couldn't help but be impressed by Cassie's obvious love for her son. Just talking about Tyler made her glow like a...well, like a Madonna. It was reassuring to know that his little nephew was being raised by such a loving and committed mother, and a doting grandfather, too. But it only made Cassie more appealing to him, *damn* it. He sat there silently, stewing over the whole situation.

"This brings me back to my original question," Cassie said, interrupting his unpleasant thoughts. "You're not happy about this, are you? Does this mean you don't want to have anything to do with Tyler?"

How did Adam answer such a question? If Tyler were *his* son, he'd sure as hell want to see the little guy. At least he *thought* that's how he'd feel... Oh, hell, he didn't know! Until Cassie showed up, having kids had been the last thing on his mind.

"You look very undecided," Cassie suggested. Before Adam could answer, she slipped a hand inside her blouse and pulled out a small snapshot. She handed it to him and he automatically took it. It was still warm from nesting against her breast and it smelled like talcum powder. But these sensations were secondary to the visceral reaction of looking at a pint-size replica of himself.

"My God," he rasped. "He looks just like—" He stopped himself. Tyler looked just like his father. His father, *Alex*. Not Adam. *Alex*.

"Handsome, isn't he?" Cassie said, her voice humming with motherly pride. "And you're right, he looks just like you, right down to the cleft in his chin."

Adam could only nod stupidly.

Then she asked, shyly, "Would you like to meet him?"

Adam swallowed hard. Of course he'd like to meet him, but that was something that could never happen. Alex had no intention of being part of his son's life, and since he, Adam, was pretending to be the boy's father, that meant he mustn't show any interest in Tyler, either.

But when he looked over the snapshot and into Cassie's hopeful eyes, Adam found he couldn't be as straightforward as he ought to be. "Well, Montana's not exactly next door. Maybe if the little guy were closer—"

Cassie's eyes shone like stars. "He *is* closer. He's in Anchorage with my father, staying at the Voyager Hotel. If you'd like to, we could fly up there tomorrow and you could meet him."

Chapter Four

Unless Adam specifically expressed an interest in meeting his son, Cassie had not intended to tell him that Tyler was in Anchorage with her father. But from the way his eyes lit up when she showed him Tyler's picture, she could have sworn he was instantly smitten. Thus the spontaneous suggestion that father and son meet. Now she wasn't so sure about Adam's reaction to the picture. Suddenly he looked more alarmed than intrigued.

"We don't have to tell him you're his daddy," Cassie quickly assured him. "And if you decide you don't want to be part of his life, I'm sure he won't remember meeting you."

Adam placed the picture on the table between them and sat back in his chair, a troubled expression on his face. "Do you want me— Do you really want Tyler's father to be part of his life, Cass? And what exactly does that mean, anyway?"

Cassie sat back, too. Her emotions were in turmoil. She wasn't sure what she wanted. And she wasn't sure why she seemed actually to be *encouraging* Adam to be part of Tyler's life. If her father were there, he'd be kicking her backside for sure. After all, Tyler was as happy as possible the way things were. She still didn't know Adam that well. What if he turned out to be a complication that Tyler could have done much better without?

"Never mind," Cassie said quickly. "It was a stupid idea."

"It wasn't a stupid idea. It's just that—"

"It should have been *your* idea," Cassie interjected, her gaze nervously flitting here, there, everywhere but at Adam. "I wasn't going to tell you Tyler was in Anchorage unless you said you wanted to meet him. But I didn't give you the chance and now you're feeling pressured and—"

Cassie was silenced when Adam gently grasped her shoulders and forced her to look at him. His expression was concerned, sympathetic. "It wasn't a stupid idea, Cass," he said succinctly. "Nothing you've thought or said or done is stupid. You're his mother. Your motives are pure and unselfish. You're only thinking of your son, which is more than I can say for the rest of us."

Cassie was torn between the pleasure of feeling his hands on her shoulders and having his face so close, and confusion at his choice of words. "The rest of us? What do you mean?"

Adam sighed, released her, sat back again. "I mean *me*. Just me. *I'm* being selfish. I'm protecting myself."

"In what way?"

"I *would* like to meet Tyler. I'm just not sure it's such a good idea."

She nodded, trying to understand. "Because

you've already decided that you don't want to be part of his life?''

"Because it would be impossible to be part of his life."

Cassie still didn't understand Adam's reasoning—in fact, he seemed almost to be hiding something—but his intentions were clear. Adam didn't plan to be part of Tyler's life.

Well, her father would be happy. As for herself, she knew she ought to be relieved, but she was actually disappointed. Maybe it was because she couldn't conceive of being a parent to a remarkable, adorable child like Tyler and not rejoicing in the fact. Even if he wasn't such a remarkable, adorable child, wasn't it normal and natural to be drawn to your own flesh and blood?

In a way, Adam's almost frightened reaction to news of Tyler's close proximity lessened her good opinion of him. Yes, as he'd said himself, it showed him to be a bit selfish. After all, if he met Tyler he might start caring for him. And caring for someone, whether it was a woman or a child, meant a certain amount of commitment. And commitment meant time and responsibilities and emotional risk. And, though she had already tried to reassure him about that, perhaps he thought it also meant *money*.

"I don't think I like what you're thinking."

Startled, Cassie looked up and into Adam's eyes.

"You think it's the money, don't you? Actually I would be more than thrilled to contribute to Tyler's upbringing and education, but I don't think you'd approve of that unless I was also part of his life.

And that's the rub. I *can't* be part of his life, Cassie."

Cassie waited, but no further explanation was offered. So, hiding her hurt, she shrugged and said, "Okay. If that's the way you want it."

"It's the way it has to be," he said, rather stubbornly, she thought. And she still didn't understand. Was there something she didn't know about the situation?

Adam knew she didn't understand, but how could he explain? He supposed he should just say he didn't want to meet Tyler because he didn't like kids, even when they were his. She could write him off as an unfeeling bastard and leave it at that. But he *did* want to meet Tyler and he wasn't an unfeeling bastard—just a lying bastard—and he was fighting the urge to tell her they'd fly up to Anchorage right after the tux fitting tomorrow.

"I'll reheat dinner," he said, forcing a cheerful tone as he stood up and moved to the counter. "You must be starved by now."

"To tell you the truth," she began, standing up, too, and turning to face him, "I'm not hungry. I wasn't hungry earlier, either. Too nervous. Now I'm just—"

"Disappointed," Adam finished for her. He could see it in her eyes. She was disappointed and, he feared, about to announce that there was no point in staying in Alaska now that she'd broken the news about Tyler. Undoubtedly it would be best if she flew back to Montana as soon as possible, but even though it would create a special kind of hell for him if she didn't, he was startled to realize how much he'd depended on her staying for the next three days.

"It's not as if I were dying to show off my new puppy or something," Cassie tried to explain. "Although I *am* tremendously proud of him. But Tyler's your *son!* From what I can see, Adam, you seem to be a pretty nice man. If I thought you were a jerk, I wouldn't even have told you about Tyler. But while I don't think you're a jerk, I *do* think you're behaving a bit like a…well, a.…"

"Coward?" he offered ruefully.

Tactfully, she did not agree, but might as well have when she continued by asking, "What are you afraid of? Or do I already know?"

She partially knew. He *was* afraid. Afraid of falling for the kid and the mother, too. Trouble was, it was more complicated than that. He had no *right* to fall for the kid or the mother. *Especially* the mother. He wasn't the man she thought he was…in oh-so-many ways! If he really were Tyler's father, he wouldn't hesitate to make plans for a trip to Anchorage. But he wasn't Tyler's father. He wasn't anybody's father. He was a phony.

Adam stared at Cassie's bleak expression, aching inside. He couldn't stand the idea of her leaving, disappointed and disgusted by him. And so he couldn't resist giving in to what they both wanted. Damn it, he'd take her to Anchorage! He'd fly up there to meet Tyler and the formidable grandfather who had once mentally tarred and feathered him. Or, rather, he'd mentally tarred and feathered Adam's twin, the original culprit. Now, in Adam's opinion, both Baranof men deserved punishment.

Although Tyler wasn't his son, he *was* his nephew, Adam continued to reason, setting aside culpability for the moment. What was the harm of getting to know and even getting to like one's own nephew? It was the mother he'd have to watch himself around. For now, however, all he cared about was making her happy again, wiping that sad look off her face.

"If I told you that we could fly up to Anchorage right after the tux fitting tomorrow morning, do you think you might get your appetite back?"

Instantly the bleakness in her eyes disappeared, but just as quickly a cautiousness crept in to tamp down the joy. "Are you sure? Or have I just forced you into doing what I want?" Her lips quirked. "Dad says I've got a way of doing that. Just like Mom."

"You've got a way about you, that's for sure," Adam acknowledged in the same rueful tone. Boy, did she ever. He had an unsettling notion that, if exposed too long to her wiles, he'd do just about anything she asked.

"No, Cassie, I actually do want to meet Tyler. However, I think, just as you suggested, it would be best if we didn't tell him I'm his father."

Cassie nodded. "Agreed. We'll just get together, the three of us, and see what happens. No expectations, no promises."

"Don't you mean the four of us?" Adam reminded her. "By the way, does your father still want to tar and feather me? He might like the result of our one-night stand, but he might still feel antipathy toward the perpetrator of the crime." It occurred to

Adam that he wouldn't mind Mr. Montgomery's ire if he'd actually had the pleasure of making love to Cassie all night long. In fact, if that were the case he wouldn't mind a lot of things.

Cassie smiled and sat down, picked up Tyler's picture and tucked it back inside her blouse. *Lucky picture.* "Like I said, Dad's settled down since I first told him I was pregnant. That was five years ago, Adam. He's not the sort of man to hold a grudge. The only way you'd get him riled up now is if he caught you doing something *new* he considered detrimental to his precious daughter."

Something new, like lying to her about who was the real father of her child?

"I think I'm hungry again," Cassie said happily. "That fish smells delicious."

Adam was glad Cassie's appetite had returned, but his had completely disappeared.

Cassie noticed that Adam didn't eat much, but then he had received quite a shock that evening. And as for conversation, she carried it while Adam pushed food around on his plate and nodded distractedly only when a response of some kind was absolutely necessary.

Finally Cassie took pity on him, stood up and dropped her napkin on the table. He gazed at her, blinking like a man just emerging from a trance. "It's getting late."

He stood, too, instantly apologetic. "I'm sorry, Cassie. I've been lousy company. Stay and have some coffee. I promise to perk up." He grinned. "No pun intended."

"Adam, I think the kindest thing I could do for

you is leave you alone so you can digest the fact that you've become a father overnight.''

"Isn't that usually the way it happens?" he teased gamely.

"It's usually not such a big surprise, and the child never arrives wearing toddler-size cowboy boots. Good night, Adam. Thanks for dinner. I'm just sorry you couldn't enjoy it, too."

"My appetite will be back by morning," he assured her, as he walked her to the door.

When he placed his hand lightly on the small of her back, ready to follow her outside, shivers ran up and down Cassie's spine. She turned, disconcerted to find his face, his lips, just inches away, and said rather breathlessly, "You don't have to escort me to my cabin, Adam. I know my way."

"A gentleman always takes his date to her door at the end of the evening," Adam insisted.

"Is this still a date?" Cassie asked, finding it hard to think while they stood so close to each other.

"I remember it starting out that way, but I feel like light-years have passed since you walked through my door at eight-thirty."

"Is that a polite way of saying I've aged you?"

He chuckled. "Just let me walk you to your cabin, Cass, if for no other reason than to protect you from the occasional bull moose, bear, or some other wild beast that might be roaming around at this hour. Remember, you're in Alaska now. You have to be a little more careful about certain things."

Cassie nodded and allowed Adam to guide her through the door, his hand still lightly pressed against her lower back. She was from Montana and not as frightened of wild beasts as Adam might think. She was much more frightened of accidentally revealing that he still did crazy things to her blood pressure and pulse. Afraid that if he bent his head to lightly kiss her on the cheek, she'd throw her arms around his neck and press her lips against his.

The night air was cool and damp and smelled of pine; and the sky, despite the fact that it was past ten o'clock at night, was the pale purple of early dusk. They accomplished the walk to the cabin in tense silence and when they reached the door, Cassie hesitated, unable to make herself turn to face him.

"Cassie?"

"Hmm?"

"Don't worry. I don't expect you to invite me in."

She turned slowly, then looked up. He smiled down at her.

"This is awkward as hell, isn't it?" he said.

"Yes. Yes, it is."

He put his hands on her shoulders, his fingers kneading her tense muscles. It felt wonderful. *Too* wonderful. "Like I said, don't worry. I'm not going to put the moves on you just because we have some history together. I know we can't pick up where we left off, and I wouldn't want to."

She winced and blushed. *"Oh."*

"No! That's not what I meant," he hurriedly explained. "Believe me, I find you very attractive…er…*still*. But things are different now."

Cassie nodded mutely. She wasn't sure she understood how he perceived the situation to be different, but she was wholeheartedly in agreement that, because of Tyler, they needed to go slowly and carefully in the romance department. Things could get even more awkward if they got involved and it didn't work out.

Of course there was always the other side of the coin...fairy-tale ending with she and Tyler and Adam becoming one big happy family. But Cassie wouldn't allow herself to entertain such an idea. While Adam might be attracted to her, he was obviously ambivalent about their son, and possibly opposed to any kind of commitment.

"You understand, don't you?"

"Do I really need to?" Cassie countered. "All that's important is that we both understand the need to avoid...well...*what happened before,* even if we both have different motivations."

Adam frowned. "It sounds like you've decided that my motivations are less than admirable."

She shrugged. "No. Since you haven't told me your motivations, I can't judge one way or the other. Maybe if you *explained—*"

His hands slid off her shoulders and fell to his sides. "I can't."

She lifted her chin. "Fine. Keep it to yourself, but I'm going to tell you my motivation, whether you want to hear it or not. I just don't want anyone getting hurt."

He reached up and gently cupped her jaw, his thumb moving in feathery circles against her skin. "Neither do I, Cass," he whispered, looking earnestly into her eyes. "Neither do I."

He turned and walked away, not looking back. Cassie chewed her bottom lip, watching with narrowed eyes until he disappeared behind some low-hanging tree branches.

What wasn't Adam telling her? What *were* his motivations? Were they purely selfish, or was he thinking of her and Tyler, too?

Who *was* he protecting, anyway?

"ALEX?"

"Oh, hi, bro." There was a pause on the other end of the line, then the whispered question, "Is something the matter?"

Adam settled in his reclining chair with the portable phone, throwing his leg over the well-padded arm. "Hell, yes, something's the matter. I didn't like this from the start and now things are worse. Cassie's brought her fath—"

"Let me call you back," Adam interrupted. "*Kelly*'s here."

Adam couldn't miss the underlying anxiety in Alex's voice. He sighed. "No, don't bother. I'm going to bed."

After another strained pause, his brother said, pointedly and in a deliberately cheerful tone, "I've told Kelly about Cassie and Tyler."

Adam sat up. "You *what*?"

"You heard me," he continued, obviously playing to an audience of one...Kelly. "With Cassie here for the wedding, it would have come out sooner or later."

"Who said you could decide that sooner was better than later?" Adam demanded to know. "Or did you spread the word early on because you figured it would make it harder for me to change my mind?"

"Cassie would have been hurt if it had been handled any other way," Alex continued. "I thought we both understood that."

Adam scowled across the room and through the window that gave back a beautiful view of wooded mountainside. Alex was right. What made him think he could take part in this deception without also lying to Kelly and every other member of the family? By claiming Tyler as his, he'd only thought at that moment of protecting Alex and making things easier for Cassie. He hadn't considered the domino effect put in motion by that first lie.

"Adam? You still there?"

"You're right," Adam conceded grimly. "Everyone should be told about *my* involvement with Cassie and *my* son. I'll tell Dad tomorrow at the tux fitting."

"Dad won't be there tomorrow."

"He won't?"

"No. He went in today to get fitted because he's got too many charters booked for tomorrow. That's why I called him an hour ago and told both him and Mom about Cassie and…and the kid."

"Don't call him 'the kid.' His name is Tyler."

"Whatever. I mean…okay."

"Weren't Mom and Dad a little surprised that the news that I'd fathered a child hadn't come from me?" Adam inquired dryly.

"I told them you were with Cassie, working things out."

"I suppose they're chomping at the bit to see their first grandchild?"

"They know that you…well…that you *may* not want to be part of his life."

"So you told them that, too? I'm sure Mom was impressed with my parental instincts."

"She didn't understand at first, but when I explained how you feel—"

"You mean how *you* feel."

"—I think they understood."

"Explain it to *me,* then, Alex," Adam muttered, "because I sure as hell don't understand not wanting to be part of your own child's life."

"What? I didn't hear you. Kelly was saying something."

"It wasn't important."

"Anyway, Kelly says she's anxious to meet Cassie and that it's too bad she didn't bring Tyler with her."

"Well…not to Seldovia."

"What do you mean…not to Seldovia?"

"Tyler's in Anchorage with his grandfather. I'm going up there tomorrow to meet him."

There was another pause, much longer this time. "You're kidding."

"No, I'm not."

In a furtive whisper, "Hell, Adam, I had no idea something like this would happen! Hold on, I'm going into the other room."

Adam waited while Alex made up some excuse to leave the room. He listened to muffled voices and fuzzy static for a couple of minutes, then Alex finally got back on the line.

"Why didn't you just tell her no?"

"Because it seemed really important to her for

me...for *Tyler's father*...to at least see his son before making any decisions about future involvement.''

''It sounds more and more like she wants you...*me*...to actually be a father to this kid.''

''His name is *Tyler*.''

''What're you doing to make her so pro fatherhood, bro? Turning on the charm?''

''Hardly. I barely spoke to her at dinner. I was shell-shocked, I guess. I think she just sees me as a decent guy and wants to be fair.''

''Well, apparently you're doing *something* to encourage her, so cut it out.''

''Maybe I should just haul off and smack her one, Alex,'' Adam drawled sarcastically. ''That's sure to make her see me in a different light.''

''Damn it, Adam, I don't know! I'm *so* sorry about all this. I really am. I know this must be tough on you. You know how grateful I am, don't you? This just wasn't something I could hit Kelly with two days before our wedding.''

''How do you know for sure? Kelly's a big girl. Maybe you're underestimating her. Maybe she'll understand. And maybe she won't care a rat's rear what her parents have to say about it.''

Alex released a long sigh. ''Adam, she told me she was glad I wasn't Tyler's father. She said it would have ruined everything.''

Adam was silenced. But only for a minute.

''It seemed like the right thing to do at the time, Alex, but now I don't know. I hate lying to Cassie.''

''It's not hurting her or anyone. else,'' Alex argued. ''Far more people would be hurt if I admitted to being Tyler's father...Cassie included. It'll be over soon, bro. She'll go home to Montana on Monday and we can forget any of this ever happened."

Easy for you to say, Adam thought to himself.

"I like her," he said, finally.

"I'm sorry about that, too," Alex answered, and Adam could hear the sincere regret in his brother's voice. "Tough luck, both of us taking a fancy to the same face. If there was any other solution..."

"What if I like Tyler just as much?"

"Like I said, someday we can forget any of this ever happened," Alex repeated, sounding just as tired and disheartened as Adam. "Go to bed, bro. Get some sleep. Tomorrow's another day."

"Right, Scarlett," Adam grumbled.

CASSIE YAWNED and stretched in the four-poster, listening to the singing of birds and humming of insects outside. Despite the tension of the night before, Cassie was surprised to feel both rested and cheerful. Though she didn't understand Adam's attitude toward Tyler and was frustrated because he wouldn't confide his feelings to her, she couldn't squelch an unexpected excitement at the prospect of introducing him to their son that day.

Cassie hadn't realized until then how much she'd missed sharing her parental pride and love for Tyler with the man who'd helped create him. Surely once the two of them met, Adam would lose his ambivalence toward their child and they'd all become friends...if nothing more.

She enjoyed a hot shower, then made a cup of Irish breakfast tea in the tiny kitchen and drank it while she dressed. Not sure what to wear to a tux-fitting, followed by a father-meets-son-for-the-first-time outing, she put on a short denim jumper embroidered on the bib, with a pink T-shirt underneath. It was casual, but it was still a dress. She applied a minimum amount of makeup and pulled her hair into a loose ponytail, tied with a pink scarf.

Since the guest house didn't have a phone, she walked up to the main cabin at eight-thirty and knocked on the door. She would have to call her father and Tyler at the hotel early, before they left on some fishing expedition, and arrange a time and location to meet.

After waiting a couple of minutes, Cassie raised her fist to knock again, but changed her mind. Adam might still be in bed. She didn't have a clue how late he normally slept and they hadn't made any plans the night before about when to start the day.

She was about to turn away and come back in half an hour when the door suddenly opened. Well, she hadn't got him out of bed.... It was worse. She'd got him out of the shower.

Chapter Five

"Hi, Cass. Sorry about this." Adam ran both hands through his wet hair and smiled sheepishly. "I couldn't relax last night and I ended up oversleeping."

Cassie tried not to stare at his chest, at the taut, glistening skin that showed through the gap of his white terry robe. She tried to keep her eyes trained to above the neck, but that didn't help her sky-rocketing blood pressure much. Freshly shaven and glowing from the shower, his chiseled cheekbones stood out magnificently. And his eyes glinted like jewels below the arch of his brows and the slicked-back Valentinolike hair.

"I...I just thought I'd better call the hotel before my dad and Tyler take off for the day," she stuttered.

He pushed open the screen door. "Good idea. Come in."

"I...I could come back later."

His lips quirked in a smile. "Why? Just get in here and make your call. Don't worry, I won't come out of the bedroom till I'm decent."

Cassie felt herself blushing as she sidled past him into the room. If not for their history together, he'd probably think her woefully naive and prudish. Or perhaps he thought so, anyway. Maybe he was only being polite last night when he told her she wasn't a klutz five years ago at the Tuddenham's bed-and-breakfast.

"Earth to Cassie."

Cassie nearly jumped. "What?"

"Did you hear me say the phone was right over there?"

He motioned toward a phone in the living room by a large, overstuffed reclining chair.

"Thanks," she mumbled, too embarrassed to look him in the eye. Unfortunately, that drew her gaze to his bare legs, descending from the bottom of his robe. Rivulets of water trailed sinuously down the well-muscled calves, which were lightly dusted with dark hair. She remembered how those legs had felt entwined with hers... Her brows furrowed. Only she didn't remember them being so well defined. Perhaps he'd been working out more in the past five years. Or running. Or—

"What's the matter, Cassie? Don't you have the phone number?"

Cassie looked up and into Adam's eyes. She wasn't sure, but she thought she detected an amused twinkle lurking there. Up came her chin. "Of course I have it. You don't think I'd put my child and my father in a hotel two hundred miles away and not know how to get in touch with them, do you?"

Adam grinned. "I didn't think so."

"What...what time should I tell Dad we can

meet? And where?'' Damn it, why did he have to be so gorgeous?

''We'll have to take the ferry to Homer, then drive to Kenai. Then we'll have to come back for the plane. We should be able to get up there by two o'clock, but since I can't be exact about the time, let's just tell your father ballpark two o'clock and meet him and Tyler at the hotel.''

''Okay.'' Cassie smiled wanly, clutched the phone against her chest and stared at him.

''I'll leave you now, so you can concentrate on what you're doing,'' he finally said, the twinkle in his eyes more apparent than ever.

Cassie was about to declare that he hadn't bothered her concentration in the least, but realized that it would make her look guilty as hell of just the opposite. Instead she turned her back on him and began to dial. She heard him pad away, then pressed the receiver button down and dialed again. Her first attempt at dialing would probably have connected her with some poor confused soul in China.

''Hello. Lone Mountain Ranch. I mean—''

''It's okay, Dad. It's me.''

''Cass. What's goin' on, honey?''

''Plenty, Dad. I told him about Tyler.''

There was a pause on the other end. ''You made up your mind about him pretty fast.''

''He's a nice guy. He'd be a good father to Tyler…if he wanted to be.''

''He doesn't want to be?''

''I don't think he knows what he wants. The whole thing was a bit of a shock. We're coming up there today so he can meet Tyler.''

"You think meetin' Tyler will help him decide what he wants?"

"I don't know, Dad. I'm confused, too."

"Well, let's not get *you-know-who* mixed up in this until you're a little less confused, okay?"

"Of course, Dad." Cassie smiled. She could hear Tyler in the background, wondering aloud if that was Mommy on the phone. "I take it *you-know-who* wants to talk to me. Have you guys been having lots of fun?"

"We're having a great time. He's in the other room eatin' some pancakes I ordered up. I don't want to put 'im on the phone till we settle this."

"Don't worry, Dad. We're not going to tell Tyler who Adam is. We'll just introduce him as a friend, or an uncle. You know, like Uncle Brad. That way if Tyler never sees him again, no big deal."

"No big deal, eh? Humph! This whole thing is a lot bigger than I wish it were. Too bad you ever got hold of that magazine, Cassie."

"Now, Dad... Let me talk to Tyler."

Cassie talked to an animated Tyler for ten minutes, listening to all the details of his first evening in Anchorage. Despite the lateness of their arrival, they'd still managed to do some fishing at a lake located within the city limits, then fried up the fish in their hotel room, which they'd chosen specifically because it had a kitchen. There was nothing Jasper and his grandson liked better than fresh skillet-fried fish.

They'd even visited Potter Marsh, apparently a game refuge, seen lots of migratory birds, a couple of beavers and a moose!

"Honey, I'm so glad you're having a good time," she said, smiling into the phone and picturing Tyler's happy face.

"When are you comin' to the hotel, Mommy? Granddad says we can go out on a boat and do some fishin' and I think you'd like that a lot, Mommy!"

"I'm coming today, Tyler."

"Really?"

"And I'm bringing a friend."

"A friend? Like my friend Justin?"

"Well, no. He's more my age. Kind of like an uncle, I guess."

"Like Uncle Brad?"

"Yes, like that. He wants to meet you and spend some time with you, too."

"Oh."

"Don't worry. He's very nice."

"Does he like t' fish?"

"Yes. I think so. We had fish for dinner last night. Now put Granddad back on the phone, Ty. I've got to arrange a time to meet you guys."

After finalizing plans with her father, Cassie said goodbye to Tyler and hung up. She turned to find Adam standing in the entryway to the hall, one shoulder resting against the doorjamb, his arms crossed over his chest. He was frowning.

"What's the matter?" Cassie asked.

"Don't tell him I'm his uncle," he said tersely. "Just say I'm a friend, okay?"

"Sure," Cassie replied quickly. "I only meant it as a sort of honorary title, you know. That's what he calls Brad."

Cassie realized the minute the name came out that

it was a mistake to mention her boyfriend back home.

"Brad? Who's Brad?"

Or maybe it wasn't a mistake...

Adam straightened up and moved into the room. He was wearing tan slacks and a forest-green sweater, the sleeves pushed up to reveal sinewy forearms.

"Just a friend of mine," Cassie said offhandedly.

"How many uncles has Ty got, Cass?" he inquired gruffly.

Cassie laughed. "You sound jealous, Adam Baranof! After forgetting my existence for five years, I find that even more mystifying than your objection to being called 'uncle'!"

Adam stared at her for a couple of minutes, his brows still lowered in a frown. Then, suddenly, he shook off his scowling demeanor and smiled. "I guess it's okay if he calls me uncle."

"Kids like to categorize the adults in their lives," Cassie explained.

"Yeah. I understand. As for being jealous, you're right, I have no business. Of course you have a life of your own back in Montana. I guess I just assumed that because you answered the ad, you were free."

"I *am* free. But, as you know, that's not why I answered the ad. I was looking for Tyler's father."

Adam shrugged and shoved his hands in his pockets. "And you found him, so I guess that closes that subject." He cocked an elbow and glanced at his watch. "We'd better get a move on. The ferry for Homer leaves in twenty minutes."

Cassie wasn't sure what to make of Adam's attitude. Part of her was pleased by what appeared to be his jealousy, but another part of her was puzzled by his objection to being called "uncle." She'd like to think it was because he really wanted Tyler to call him "Daddy," but just wasn't ready to admit it yet. As she followed him to the car—irresistibly admiring the view of a tight rear and long legs—she smiled to herself and allowed a smidgen of hope to blossom.

Careful, Cassie, she told herself. *Don't start getting dewy-eyed about this guy. At least not with so little to go on.*

Fortunately it was another clear, beautiful day and Cassie was able to distract herself from the scenery inside the Jeep with the scenery outside the Jeep. Seldovia was charming. Most of the timber houses were on pilings and the town proper was highlighted by a picturesque boardwalk that, according to Adam, dated back to the 1930s. They stopped at the Two Sisters Bakery to pick up muffins and coffee to go, then headed for the ferry dock.

"How many people live here?" Cassie asked as she peered curiously around and nibbled on her muffin.

"Four hundred or so. Fishing, timber and tourism supports most of the residents. Then there's guys like me and Alex who just like it here. We're away a lot, though."

With a wave at the man standing inside the pay booth, Adam drove the Jeep onto the ferry.

"Away doing what?"

"We both do some teaching at Fairbanks University and at the university extensions scattered around the state. I get a few research grants and am frequently on-site for that, and Alex does a lot of contracted work for the petroleum companies. When he and Kelly move to Florida, though, they'll both work full-time for the same company. They'll still be required to travel a lot, though, mostly to the Middle East.''

''No more teaching?''

Adam parked, pressed the security brake, finished off the last of his muffin, then helped Cassie out of the Jeep. ''Alex is too ambitious to teach. It doesn't make enough money. And he can't stand staying in one place for too long. He's looking forward to the traveling.''

''He's lucky he found a woman who shares his views and his talents. They seem very compatible.''

''They are.''

''What about children?''

Adam had taken her arm and was leading her to the railing that faced north toward Kachemac Bay, holding his coffee in his free hand. She felt his fingers spasm, momentarily tighten around her elbow, then gradually relax. ''What do you mean?''

She tried to catch his eye, but his gaze remained fixed on the bay. He squinted into the sunshine and the cool breeze off the water, sipping his coffee.

''Are they planning to have kids? All that traveling might be hard to do with kids in the picture.''

''Alex and Kelly aren't interested in having a family right now. Not now, and maybe not ever. As I told you, they're both very career-oriented. Kids simply don't figure in.''

Cassie nodded. ''Then I guess it was a good thing

you're Tyler's father and not Alex. Even if he chose not to have anything to do with Tyler, Kelly might have freaked out a little…you know?''

He turned, gazed at her briefly, then said, ''Yeah. I suppose that's possible.''

''Have you talked to Alex since last night? Did he tell anyone about…about me and Tyler?''

''Yes, I have talked to Alex. I hope you don't mind, but he did tell Kelly and our parents about you and Tyler.'' He watched her and waited.

Cassie raised her brows. ''*I* certainly don't mind, but I'm a little surprised. I didn't think you'd want your parents to know about us unless you'd decided to be part of Tyler's life.''

''I didn't give Alex permission to tell everyone, he just did,'' Adam admitted.

Cassie's stomach knotted up. ''In other words, you're sorry he told them.''

''No, that's not it, Cassie,'' Adam said with a sigh, looking earnestly into her eyes. ''It's just that—like you said—maybe I would have kept quiet at least until I'd decided what I wanted to do about Tyler.''

Cassie nodded. His reasoning was sound and sensible. He was behaving the way most men would in such a situation. Actually *better* than most men. She certainly couldn't blame him for that. And, if he was a little uptight this morning, she knew he was probably just nervous about meeting Tyler and her father.

As they approached Homer Spit, Kachemac Bay turned into a veritable hubbub of maritime activity. Fishing boats, sailboats, motorboats and ferries came and went. Overhead and on the shore seabirds of every description screamed and chattered. Adam pointed out a bald eagle sailing high above the spruce trees that lined the shore. When Cassie smiled in delight, he slipped his arm in hers and leaned close, suddenly seeming far from uptight.

"There's an eagle's nest near my house in Seldovia. I'll have to show it to you before you leave."

His breath against her ear thrilled Cassie, and her heart fluttered like a schoolgirl's. She wondered why Adam did that to her, and why Brad didn't. Especially since Brad was the one who stuck around and Adam was the one that got away. She wondered, did he always make a point of getting away?

Homer was bigger than Seldovia, but just as charming. The long narrow gravel bar that was the "spit" was lined with visitor shops, eateries, art galleries, commercial wharfs, docks for waterborne sight-seeing and fishing cruises, parking places, campsites and a port for the huge oceangoing ferry, the *Tustumena*.

"I'd show you my dad's boat, but he's already out on his first charter," Adam said. He drove slowly through the tiny town, pointing out sights of interest, then took the Sterling Highway to Kenai.

Minutes later, they were entering Harold's Tux Towne. Still dazzled by the bright sunshine and the way it glinted off the water that had seemed to greet them at every turn in the road, Cassie had to blink a few times before her eyes became adjusted to the artificial light inside the formal-wear shop.

When she could focus, the first sight to greet her

was Adam looking dashing in a black tuxedo. No, that couldn't be Adam, that had to be—

"Hi, Cassie. I want you to meet my fiancée, Kelly. Kelly, this is Cassie."

Cassie was shocked all over again at how exactly alike Adam and his twin were. It took her a minute to drag her gaze away from Alex to look at his fiancée.

Kelly was a tall woman, slim, auburn-haired and beautiful. Her expression was friendly but cautious, and Cassie couldn't help but feel that she might harbor a bit of suspicion about her. Possibly she was simply feeling protective toward her soon-to-be brother-in-law and was hoping Adam wasn't being taken in by a floozy. Of course, all of this was mere speculation. Or paranoia!

"Hi, Cassie." Kelly extended her slim hand and gave Cassie's a firm, feminine shake. "It's nice to meet you."

Cassie smiled wryly. "But a bit awkward, isn't it? I'm sure you don't have any idea what to say to me."

Kelly's chuckle sounded relieved. "I'm glad you said that. You're right. I wasn't sure what to say. I didn't know whether to bring up your little boy or not."

"Please do," Cassie said, her chin raising automatically. "I love talking about my son."

"Alex says you're going up to Anchorage today so Adam can meet him." Her gaze shifted to Adam, who was standing behind Cassie and had so far said nothing. "That should be...er...fun."

Cassie waited for Adam to say something. How

he spoke of Tyler around his friends and family could make or break her good opinion of him. She'd be very upset if he acted embarrassed or ashamed.

Adam rested a hand on Cassie's shoulder. "I'm looking forward to meeting Tyler," he said. "Judging by his picture and the twinkle in his mother's eyes every time she talks about him, he's quite a kid. I'm glad she brought him to Alaska with her."

Adam spoke with a firmness and conviction that delighted Cassie and filled her heart with gratitude. She turned and smiled up at Adam, hoping to convey how very admirably he'd risen to the occasion.

When Cassie turned and smiled at him, Adam was nearly knocked over by an onslaught of emotions. She was glowing, her eyes shining, her lips trembling ever so slightly at the corners. His heart swelled with tenderness and he wanted to take her in his arms and hold her close. But he couldn't. He had no right. She was only feeling gratitude toward him for behaving like *Alex* should have been behaving. As it was, both brothers were first-class jerks, only Cassie didn't know that. Sweet Cassie was too damned trusting for her own good.

"When are you going up?" Alex asked, breaking the odd mix of tension in the room. Adam looked at his brother, seeing the barely contained anxiety behind his bland expression. He probably couldn't wait to get rid of them, but didn't dare show it.

Again Adam felt an unwilling surge of sympathy for his brother. He gave Alex a brotherly punch in the arm, something they frequently resorted to as a show of affection that wouldn't embarrass them at the same time. "We're leaving right after I try on that monkey suit you expect me to wear at the wedding. If I'd known being best man was going to be so uncomfortable, I might have bailed out.''

''That's a bunch of baloney, bro,'' Alex said. ''You'd never bail out on me.''

Adam didn't answer, didn't meet his brother's searching gaze.

''Did you bring Tyler's picture with you, Cassie?'' Kelly suddenly inquired. ''I'd love to see what he looks like.''

Cassie's face lit up even brighter than before. ''Of course I brought a picture. I take one with me everywhere.'' This time, instead of pulling it out of her blouse, Cassie took the picture out of her purse. She handed it to Kelly and Alex peered at it over his fiancée's shoulder.

''Oh, my gosh, he looks just like you, Adam,'' Kelly exclaimed. ''Right down to the Baranof cleft in his chin. Doesn't he look like your brother, Alex? Isn't he adorable?''

Adam watched the play of emotions on his brother's face. Surprise, confusion, fear. ''Yeah. He's the spitting image of his father all right.'' His gaze flicked up to meet Adam's. Like most twins, they were very tuned to each other's thoughts and feelings. But, for once in his life, Adam didn't have a clue what was going on in his brother's head. Was it possible that a bit of fatherly feeling and paternal pride had surfaced?

While Adam watched and tried to analyze Alex's reaction to seeing his son for the first time, Harold, the diminutive, balding owner of the shop, bustled up to him with a tuxedo shrouded in a plastic bag draped over his arm. He led Adam away to the dressing room, all the while lamenting over the Baranof twins' broad shoulders and what they might do to the seams of his tuxedo jackets.

Alex followed them into the dressing room, but with Harold hovering and assisting and dictating, there was no opportunity for the brothers to speak privately.

Finally trussed up in his tux, Adam emerged from the dressing room to stand before the triple mirrors alongside Alex. In the mirror's reflection he saw Kelly and Cassie talking animatedly at the other side of the store where they'd left them.

"I wonder what they're talking about?" Alex said nervously.

Adam waited until Harold moved away to greet another customer, then answered, "Probably about something that has nothing to do with you or me. Don't panic."

Alex sighed. "My nerves were bad enough just getting ready for the wedding. Now *this.*"

Adam tugged on the cuffs of his shirtsleeves and looked at Alex's eyes in the mirror. "Lying is very stressful, but it doesn't have to be this way. It's not too late to come clean."

"Are you crazy? Coming clean is the last thing I want to do."

"Even after seeing Tyler's picture?"

Alex grimaced. "What do you mean by that?"

"Didn't you feel anything when you looked at the picture?"

"Oh, I felt *something*. I was shocked that he really does look just like me. Is that what you mean?"

Adam knew that if he had to explain to Alex what a father might feel when looking at the spitting image of himself, there was really no point in going into it. You either felt something or you didn't. He was rather amazed, though, that *he'd* felt something and Alex hadn't.

"Wow. God was in a good mood when he made you two," Kelly said as she and Cassie approached. "Two more gorgeous men I've never set eyes on before."

Alex did some playful preening for his fiancée and kissed her cheek, but Adam quickly changed the subject. "What were you ladies talking about?" He looked at Cassie, but she didn't answer. She just kept gazing back and forth between him and Alex, her expression thoughtful.

Kelly just ignored the question, still in a mood to tease and flatter. "Yep. Since you came as a matched pair, it's a good thing you're easy on the eyes. You know, sometimes when you two are dressed alike, I can hardly tell you apart."

Cassie looked interested. "You mean there are times you actually *can* tell them apart? How?"

"Well, there's a slight difference in their builds for one thing. Adam's a runner, so his calves are more developed, but that doesn't help when he's wearing long pants. Another way to tell is by their hands and the way they use them. For example, if you tied Alex's hands behind his back, he wouldn't be able to talk." Kelly got a coy look on her face and ran her hand over Alex's chest. "Then there's the difference between their—"

Alex gave Adam a warning look in the mirror.

"Kelly, don't give away all our secrets," Adam said with a forced chuckle. "And, speaking of secrets, are you or are you not going to tell us what you two were talking about while I was being manhandled in the dressing room?"

Kelly grinned. "Girl talk."

"That sounds ominous," Alex said with a nervous chuckle.

"Oh, it's nothing *bad,* Alex. It's something I think the whole family will appreciate."

"Don't keep us in suspense, Kelly," Adam prompted.

"You tell him, Cassie," Kelly invited.

Adam looked at Cassie, who appeared to be teeter-tottering between feelings of excitement and doubt. "I hope you'll think this is okay, Adam."

A feeling of dread he knew Alex shared swelled in Adam's chest. He smiled encouragingly. "Just spit it out, Cass."

She wrung her hands and tried to smile back. "Well...Kelly's been nice enough to invite Tyler and my father to the wedding, too. She wants us to bring them back with us when we fly to Anchorage. Is...is that okay with you, Adam?"

Chapter Six

Out of the corner of his eye Adam saw Alex stiffen. He could feel his brother's anxiety on a visceral level and, combined with his own, that was a pretty miserable sensation. Things were getting way out of hand.

"I've asked too much," Cassie suggested. Her voice was calm, she was half-smiling, but Adam could see the blossoming hurt in her eyes.

"No, Cass. Not at all," Adam immediately assured her, feeling like a bone in a tug-of-war between starving dogs, about to be torn in two. He knew Alex didn't want to see Tyler, much less have the little guy, his mother and his grandfather attending the wedding! What a nightmare!

On the other hand, Cassie would be devastated if Adam refused to bring them down for the wedding. It would clearly imply that he saw his son as an unwanted intrusion into his life, his family. It would make Cassie think he was ashamed of Tyler. Ashamed of his and Cassie's night together.

And that simply wasn't true. *If* he'd slept with Cassie five years ago, *if* he really was Tyler's father, he wouldn't hesitate to bring them down from Anchorage to meet the entire Baranof clan. And since he was doing Alex a favor by standing in for him as both ex-lover and father, he decided that *he'd* make the decision without worrying overly much about how uncomfortable it would make his twin brother. In fact, maybe it would be good for Alex to feel a little uncomfortable...

"I think it's a great idea, Cass," Adam told her, then watched as her face lit up. He loved the way every feeling, sad or happy, was reflected in those beautiful gray eyes of hers. He thought he heard a small gasp coming from Alex's direction, but he refused to look at his twin, finding it much more enjoyable to gaze at an honest face over one racked with guilt and fear. He refused to look at his own reflection for the same reason.

"You're sure?" she murmured.

Kelly chuckled and leaned close to Cassie to whisper in her ear, "Don't give him a chance to change his mind!"

"I won't change my mind," Adam stated. "It's a done deal, Cassie."

She smiled her pleasure.

"Isn't this great, Alex?" Kelly chirped, slipping her arm in his and leaning against his side. "Most of my brothers and sisters and their families are flying in from Florida, your huge family is ferrying and flying in from all parts of Alaska, and, to cap it all, there'll be surprise guests from Montana! Heck, we'll have the whole fam-damily at the wedding!" She laughed. "That is, unless *you've* got an adorable little son stashed away somewhere I don't know about. But in that situation I think I might feel just a *teensy* bit less inclined to extend an invitation. Not to mention, Dad would have a cow!''

The others chuckled halfheartedly at Kelly's attempted joke, but no one looked particularly amused. Adam knew why he and Alex weren't busting a gut, and he was pretty sure he knew why Cassie wasn't laughing, either. As any mother would be, she was sensitive to any suggestion that Tyler was somehow unacceptable because of the circumstances of his birth. Sure, it was okay with Kelly as long as *Adam* was Ty's father. But if it was *Alex*...

Adam decided that it was time to leave. Ignoring his brother's pale, shell-shocked appearance, he summoned Harold, hurried along the final fussings over his tuxedo, quickly changed into his street clothes and ushered Cassie to the Jeep.

Kelly waved from the door as they sped away toward Sterling Highway.

''She's really nice,'' Cassie said, waving back and looking over her shoulder through the window until they'd turned a corner.

''You still think so despite that bit about feeling less inclined to invite a child that belonged to Alex?'' Adam inquired dryly. ''That wasn't very tactful of her.''

Cassie settled in her seat and turned toward him with a thoughtful expression. ''No, it wasn't tactful. But she wasn't intentionally trying to hurt or offend me.''

''No, I'm sure it wasn't intentional,'' Adam conceded.

''I certainly didn't expect her to invite my father

and Tyler to the wedding,'' Cassie continued thoughtfully. Her face brightened. ''It's going to be great to have Ty with me for the weekend. I miss him even when we're only separated for a day.'' Her smile broadened, became coy. ''You'll find out what I mean, Adam. You're going to love him.''

Adam nodded, swallowed, smiled weakly. That's what he was afraid of.

She cocked her head to the side, watching his reaction with interest. ''Does this mean you've changed your mind about not wanting to be part of Tyler's life?''

Adam sighed and looked at the road. ''I'm not sure what this means, Cass. We'll just have to wait and see.''

WE'LL JUST have to wait and see. Those words kept swirling through Cassie's mind during the entire trip to Anchorage, teasing her, tempting her to hope that Adam wasn't going to vanish from their lives like he had before. She didn't try to analyze her feelings, to separate her desire for Tyler to know and benefit from a father's influence and her own very grown-up desires of the heart. As Adam had said, she'd just wait and see what developed. She was a mature adult and she could handle it if, while being a father to their son, Adam only wanted to be friends with her. At least she was pretty sure she could.

Sometimes she thought of Brad and felt guilty. Not guilty because her heart was being unfaithful to him—he'd never really captured her heart, nor had she given it—but guilty because she couldn't feel about him after three years the way it would be so easy to feel about Adam in four minutes.

"What are you thinking about, Cassie?" Adam inquired as they began their descent onto Lake Hood.

Cassie automatically answered, "Brad."

Adam raised a brow and gave a half smile. "I see."

No, you don't, Cassie thought. But she didn't dare explain everything she'd been thinking and why, or he'd definitely run for the hills!

They reached the Voyager Hotel that afternoon by one-thirty and headed straight to the room where Tyler and her dad were staying. With a mother's pride and confidence, she knew Adam wouldn't be able to help falling in love with Tyler. Most people liked her dad, too...once they got past his prickly facade. She just hoped her Montana men took to Adam as quickly as she had.

"This is it," Cassie said as they reached room 230 and paused outside the door.

"Yep," Adam answered laconically.

"You're nervous," Cassie stated, suddenly noticing how strained he appeared. She'd been so caught up in her own excitement and happy hopes, she hadn't noticed Adam's deteriorating composure until just then. Oh, most people wouldn't think he was nervous at all. He wasn't fidgeting or shifting or pacing. He was standing perfectly still. But there was a tiny furrow between his eyes she'd never noticed before and a barely perceptible muscle ticking in his jaw. That muscle had been ticking the night before, just after he'd found out he was a father.

Adam smiled, but Cassie could tell it was done with an effort. "Sure, I'm nervous," he said finally. "I'd be some kind of a hard case if I weren't."

"You've got a point," Cassie agreed with a sympathetic nod, then turned and rapped lightly on the door. "But try not to worry too much. I have a feeling all three of you guys are going to hit it off."

Adam wasn't so sure about the "all three" part of Cassie's prediction, but he nodded and smiled anyway. A second later the door creaked open about four inches and, toward the very top of it, a large nose and a long gray handlebar mustache poked out. "That you, Cass?" a gruff voice asked in a whisper.

Cassie chuckled. "Yes, Dad," she whispered back. "You were expecting maybe the mob?"

The door opened a few more inches. Pale eyes in a leathered face rested on Cassie, warming to an azure blue as he smiled down at her. Those same eyes, as they turned on Adam, became as cool and steely as gunmetal.

"I don't have to ask who you are," he announced in a slightly sarcastic drawl. "The boy couldn't look more like you if he'd been cloned."

"So I hear," Adam replied, careful not to allow his gaze to shift away from the older man's piercing scrutiny. He extended a hand. "I'm happy to meet you."

Jasper Montgomery stared down at Adam's hand for a protracted couple of seconds, then he extended his own hand and the two men shook. *Score one for me,* thought Adam. *I didn't back down and he didn't refuse to shake.*

"Why are we standing in the hall, Dad?" Cassie

asked, her voice tinged with amusement. "And why are we all whispering?"

"The boy's asleep," Jasper announced, opening the door and standing to the side. "The sunlight and the excitement got him confused last night and he didn't doze off till the wee hours. 'Fraid it's all caught up with him this afternoon. He's been down for a couple of hours, though, so I expect it wouldn't hurt to wake 'im up now."

Adam followed Cassie into the hotel room, down a hallway past the bathroom to an open suite containing bedroom and kitchenette. There in the middle of the room in the middle of a king-size bed lay a pint-size boy. He was flat on his back, sprawled like a starfish, his arms and legs flung away from his body. On second thought, with his cowboy boots still on and his hat on the nearby pillow, Adam decided he looked more like a star of an old-time western than a starfish, staked out by the black-hatted villains in the middle of the desert to die of sunstroke and ant bites.

But more than that, Tyler looked like Alex. And he looked like *him*. And, strangely enough, he was sleeping in Adam's favorite childhood sleeping position! Uncontained and comfortable, Adam had paid no attention to his brother in the same double bed, leaving Alex to sleep clinging to his own narrow portion of the mattress on the very edge.

"My God," Adam whispered under his breath. Cassie was standing beside the bed, gazing down at Tyler, but Adam had stopped a few feet away, stunned and immobile.

"Hadn't you seen a picture of 'im?" Jasper

asked. He stood on the other side of the bed, opposite Cassie. He peered narrowly at Adam from under bushy brows.

"Yes. Yes, and I could see the resemblance then. But seeing him in person..." Adam's voice trailed off. He couldn't help himself; he added, "And he sleeps just like I used to sleep, hogging the whole bed."

"Yep, he's a helluva bed partner," Jasper agreed with a proud sniff. "Always was."

"You really slept like this, too, Adam?" Cassie asked, her eyes wide with delighted interest. "Gosh, I wonder how many ways you two are alike?"

This brought Adam up short. Yes, how many ways were Tyler and his *uncle* alike? It stood to reason that some of Adam's traits had found their way into Tyler's personality. But it also stood to reason that he'd have more traits in common with Alex.

"Come closer, Adam," Cassie urged, waving him over. "He won't bite. At least not while he's asleep."

Tentatively, Adam obeyed. He walked slowly to Cassie's side of the bed and joined her in the decidedly mommy-and-daddylike activity of watching a child sleep. Who else would find such a way of passing time anything but extremely boring?

But Adam wasn't bored. God help him, he was enthralled. The child, who was no doubt a ball of fire while awake, looked like an angelic choirboy in sleep. Long, thick lashes lay against round, flushed cheeks. His lips were tilted, almost smiling, above a stubborn chin with a deep dimple that would someday be the Baranof cleft.

"He's dreamin' of fishin'," Jasper theorized. "Or flyin'. I used to dream of flyin' all the time when I was a kid."

"Well, let's wake him up and let him experience the real thing," Cassie said, bending over the bed to carefully trail her fingers through the thick, dark hair that fell over Tyler's forehead.

"What d'ya mean?" Jasper immediately demanded to know.

Cassie looked up at her father, smiling. "Adam's flying us down to Seldovia. We're all three going to stay at his house and attend his brother's wedding."

Quick as a trigger finger, Jasper turned those steely eyes in Adam's direction, full of suspicion. "We are? How come?"

"My brother's fiancée extended the invitation just this morning," Adam explained, feeling a bit sheepish. Jasper had every reason to be suspicious, to wonder what was in the works.

"They all know about Tyler…about you and Cass?"

"They will by the end of the weekend," Adam answered. "So far, only my brother, his fiancée and my parents know."

Jasper cocked a brow. "Your parents, eh? Well, what do they think about the sudden appearance of a grandchild?"

"Frankly, sir, I don't know. I haven't talked to them yet. It was my twin brother who—"

Now both brows flew up. "Your brother's a *twin*?" His keen eyes flitted to Cassie, then back to

Adam. ''Then how the hell does Cassie know which of the two of you is Tyler's real father?''

Adam's stomach felt like a dishrag being twisted in the hands of a hefty housewife. His heart was drumming in his ears and he felt as close to fainting as the day when he was ten years old and he'd buried a fishhook an inch deep in his thumb.

Cassie's easy laugh partially revived him. ''Dad, how can you ask such a question?'' she said with a mildly scolding look. ''I know Adam's the father because he told me so.''

Jasper grunted. ''Yeah, but when you got his reply in the mail, he didn't remember you.''

''Not at first. But he remembers everything now.''

''That true, son?'' Jasper looked at him until Adam felt as if the old man could see right through to the troubled soul inside. It was obvious this Montana rancher was as canny as a coyote. He didn't miss much, that's for sure.

Adam was close to spilling everything. He wanted to. He wanted to in the worst way. But he'd promised his brother to protect his wedding day and if he intended to renege on that promise Alex should be the first to know what his intentions were. Such being the case, the first thing Adam would do when he got back to Seldovia was corner Alex and talk sense to him, hopefully talk him into coming clean. Together they could confess and throw themselves on the mercy of the women. Cass and Kelly could then decide what the lying Baranof twins deserved.

''Dad, I'm sure Adam doesn't appreciate being grilled,'' Cassie said, looking worriedly at Adam, then back to her father. She blushed. ''Believe me,

I know he remembers that night because…because he mentioned something very particular and personal about me that he couldn't possibly have guessed.''

Jasper grunted again, spun on his boot heels and stalked to the kitchen mumbling something about "more than he needed to know."

Adam sighed with relief. He was saved for now, but the reckoning was coming. He wanted it to come. He was hating this deceit more and more. Cassie was just too trusting. She was apparently so honest herself she was incapable of being suspicious of others' dishonesty.

"Adam?"

Adam had been gazing down at Tyler, fighting that recurring idea that everything would be just fine if only he really were the boy's father. He looked up at Cassie. "Thanks for coming to my rescue."

"Listen, don't worry about Dad. He'll come around. He's just very protective of me and Tyler." She smiled. "Maybe when we get to Seldovia you can show all three of us that eagle's nest."

"If you can wake up Tyler," Adam teased. "The kid sleeps like a rock." Just like he used to. A brass band could be marching through the room and it wouldn't wake him.

But when Cassie leaned down and whispered in Tyler's ear, "Wake up, sleepyhead," he blinked open his eyes and sat up, as alert as if cymbals had crashed over his head. Tyler was just like him in that respect, too. Once awakened, Adam was instantly alert.

"Mommy? Mommy, you're back!"

Adam watched as Tyler threw his arms around Cassie's neck. Mother and child obviously had a great relationship. He'd known that all along, of course, but now he was seeing it in the flesh.

Cassie sat down on the bed and drew Tyler next to her, hip to hip. She looked up at Adam, and Tyler followed her gaze. Soft gray eyes and bright blue ones were staring up at him, their ingenuous and trusting expressions almost identical. It was damned unsettling. "Honey, I want you to meet my friend, Adam. You know the one I told you about over the phone?"

Tyler rubbed one eye with a fist and nodded. "Hello, Uncle Adam."

"No, Tyler," Cassie said quickly, "just call him—"

"I told you it was okay, Cass. Remember? *Uncle* Adam's fine," Adam stated. "Pleased to meet you, Tyler." Cassie looked uncertain at first, but Adam's smile and shrug reassured her that he really had changed his mind and was okay with the honorary title. Even if his true relationship was thrown in his face every time Tyler said his name, Adam figured it was no more than he deserved. He just hoped that Jasper—who was watching them from the kitchen with a grim expression on his weathered face, his lanky frame propped against the counter—wouldn't notice that every time Tyler used the avuncular term, Adam had to fight the inclination to cringe.

"Do you like t' fish?" Tyler immediately wanted to know.

"Love to. Do you like salmon?"

"I like trout th' best, but salmon's good 'nd it's bigger, too."

"I know a great place where you can catch salmon that's twice your size, Tyler."

His eyes lit up. "Really? When can we go?"

Cassie laughed. "As soon as you and your grand-dad are packed."

"Cass, can I have a word with you…er…*over here?*" Jasper called from the kitchen area. He was speaking to Cassie, of course, but he was looking at Adam with the expression of a man about to round up a posse.

"If you two want to talk in private, I can wait downstairs in the lobby," Adam offered, already headed for the door.

"No." Cassie stepped in front of him, putting her hands on his chest. The contact seemed to startle them both at first and for a couple of seconds they simply stood there, staring into each other's eyes.

Adam glanced at Jasper. He was looking more and more in the mood for a lynching. "I don't mind, Cass. Really."

Cassie glanced at Jasper, too, removed her hands and nervously clasped them behind her. "It would be more efficient time-wise for Dad and I to talk while I walk him down to the lobby to pay the hotel bill and check out. You wouldn't mind staying with Tyler for a few minutes, would you? He's always hungry when he gets up from a nap. Maybe you could fix him something to eat. I'm sure Dad's got something in the cupboard for snack attacks."

While Adam hesitated, wondering how to reply, Tyler slipped off the bed and moved to stand by his mother. "I am hungry," he admitted. "Granddad bought some peanut butter 'nd jelly at the store." He pointed at Adam. "Can he make sand'iches?"

"I'd be surprised if he couldn't," Cassie answered, her hand resting on the back of Tyler's head. "He's a very good cook. He makes fish almost as delicious as Granddad's."

Adam tried to look humble as Tyler gazed up at him with a new respect. He realized Cassie's endorsement might be good for *him,* but Jasper might not appreciate competition in the sacred fish-cooking category.

"Okay," Tyler said. "Let's go, Uncle Adam." And with that he headed for the kitchen, smiling up at his grandfather as he passed, seemingly completely unaware of the tension in the room. Jasper smiled back and tousled his grandson's hair. It was only during that brief expression of affection for his grandson that the scowl left Jasper's face for even a nanosecond.

"I guess I'll be making sandwiches while you guys check out," Adam announced, meeting Jasper's fierce gaze unblinkingly as he followed Tyler into the kitchen. He realized that the best way to handle Jasper was probably by not showing fear. And he really wasn't intimidated by the stern old man, anyway. He understood and empathized with his feelings and suspicions completely. What Adam was really feeling to the point of misery was guilt.

"See you in a few minutes, Tyler, Adam. Come on, Dad," Cassie called from the door. "The sooner we get you guys checked out, the sooner Tyler can get his first floatplane ride."

Tyler stopped in the middle of licking peanut butter off his thumb. ''Flying? We're going *flying?*'' he squeaked.

Cassie grinned. ''Yep.''

''In another plane?''

''I hear it's the only way to go,'' Cassie answered solemnly, her eyes sparkling. ''But I'll let Uncle Adam tell you all about his plane. Bye, hon.''

When the door finally closed behind Cassie and her father, Adam looked down and found a peanut-butter-smeared face gazing up at him expectantly. ''Well, Uncle Adam? Are ya goin' t' tell me about your plane or not?''

''WHAT WAS that all about?'' Jasper nearly shouted as soon as they'd walked ten feet down the hall in the direction of the elevators.

Cassie slipped her hand around her father's elbow and smiled determinedly. ''What was what all about, Dad?''

Exasperated, Jasper stopped in his tracks and flung an arm in the direction of room 230. ''*That!* What was *that* all about? Are you crazy leaving Tyler with a total stranger?''

Cassie crossed her arms over her chest and faced him. ''Adam's no stranger. Adam is his father.''

''Well, that may be true, but—''

''What do you mean *may* be true? I told you he knows something about me that's quite personal and—''

Jasper lifted both hands, palms forward. ''Never mind. I don't want to know. What I *do* want to know is why you're acting so featherbrained and teachin' Tyler all kinds of wrong lessons?''

Cassie angled a brow. "Featherbrained?"

"As a peahen. Why else would you leave your son alone with a man he just met?"

"Is that what you mean by teaching wrong lessons?"

"He'll be going to school soon, Cass. Do you want him to think he can hobnob with just anybody off the street?"

"That's not going to happen, Dad, and you know it. Tyler knows I approve of him staying with Adam and that's the only reason he's comfortable doing it. He realizes that I trust Adam."

"And why *is* that? Why do you trust him? We've been in Alaska less than twenty-four hours and this fella's apparently won you over already. Hell, doesn't this cozy scenario seem just a little too familiar to ya, Cass?"

Cassie felt her face heating up. She waited until a couple passed them in the hall, then said in a lowered voice, "Dad, you aren't implying that I—that Adam and I—"

"Not implyin'. Askin'. Have ya done the mattress dance with 'im, Cass?"

Cassie laughed, embarrassed, indignant and amused at the same time. "Where on earth did you pick up that phrase? I think you've been watching too many talk shows, Dad."

"Bah! You're being evasive."

Cassie sighed. "Come on, let's walk while we talk." She took his arm and they proceeded again toward the elevators.

"Are you going to answer my question or not?" he persisted.

"Yes, Dad, I—"

She could feel him stiffen. "You mean you actually *did*—"

"Listen to me. Yes, I *am* going to answer your question."

"Oh."

"And *no*, I haven't slept with Adam. I told you things would be different this time and…and they are. Actually, in many ways *he* seems different this time."

They reached the elevator bank and her father pushed the Down button. He gazed at her thoughtfully. "But you are attracted to him, aren't you? I can see it, Cass, so don't even try to deny it."

Cassie returned her father's gaze directly. "Yes, I'm attracted to him, but I'm trying very hard not to let it influence the way I handle his and Tyler's relationship. I'm trying to be objective."

Jasper snorted. "Hell, honey, I don't think you *can* be objective."

She poked him in the chest. "Apparently neither can you. And while I think that partially has to do with your protective feelings toward me and Tyler, I also think you're thinking of Brad."

Jasper's brows lowered. Soberly, he asked, "What about Brad?"

Cassie shook her head, just as sober. "Dad, you know I care about Brad—"

"But?"

"I know you love him like a son, and Tyler adores him."

"But?"

"But after three years you'd think I'd have married the guy by now. Bottom line, we just weren't meant to be. When we get back to Montana I'm going to have to tell him how I feel so he can get on with his life."

Cassie felt like a villain. Her father's face showed how terribly disappointed he was. "You've never talked this way before. You've never let on that there was no hope at all of you and Brad getting together."

She shrugged helplessly. "I guess it took this trip to make me see the truth."

He shook his head. "That scares the hell out of me."

"Why?"

"For the same reason it scares you, I expect. It's Adam. In just a day, you like *him* better than Brad."

Cassie nodded. Earlier that day, she'd been thinking the same thing.

"Where's this goin', Cass?"

She gave a helpless chuckle. "I wish I knew." She hesitated, then continued, "Dad, you know I respect and appreciate your opinions—"

"I should hope so."

"—but if you're not objective about Adam your opinion isn't worth much, is it?"

He grimaced. "No, I guess not."

"Besides, he *is* Tyler's father. Isn't that reason enough to give the guy a chance?"

The elevator pinged and the doors opened.

"I guess so," he agreed grudgingly as they stepped into the elevator. He gave her a quick kiss on the cheek and faced forward. "But being objective doesn't mean I'm not allowed to watch 'im like a hawk."

Cassie also turned to face the closing doors. "I know, Dad," she said ruefully. "I know."

Chapter Seven

During the twenty minutes Cassie and Jasper left him alone with Tyler, Adam got to know a lot about his nephew. He learned that he made a pretty mean peanut butter and jelly "sand'ich" all by himself, but didn't like eating alone. Adam hated the gooey consistency of peanut butter, but he gagged down half a sandwich anyway just to be sociable.

He learned that Tyler refused to eat jam with seeds in it because the seeds stuck between his teeth. He said it felt kind of like having sand in his mouth like when he fell off his horse, Buster, last year. No, he didn't break anything, just got a "gritty mouthful" as Granddad said. He didn't cry, either. He wasn't a crybaby, he informed Adam proudly, not even when he got shots at the doctor's.

Next to fishing, his favorite thing to do was listen to stories about animals, especially big ones like elephants and dinosaurs and whales. His four favorite people were Mommy, Granddad, Sylvie and Uncle Brad.

Someday Mommy and Uncle Brad were going to get married and he was going to have little brothers.

No sisters, just brothers. No, Mommy never said so, but he just had a feelin' that someday Uncle Brad was going to end up being his daddy. He'd never had a dad before, you know. By the way, did Uncle Adam have any Jolly Ranchers in his pocket?

By now Adam was beginning to realize that although Cassie had claimed to be free of romantic entanglements back home, this Brad fella had to be a pretty big part of their lives. He was certainly important to Tyler. And while he also realized that once Cassie found out he'd lied about being Tyler's father there was little to no chance of having a relationship with her. He was so jealous of Brad his jaw ached from clenching it at the thought of her kissing some Montana cowboy who probably looked like Kevin Costner in *Silverado*... you know, romantically heroic. Or like Michael Landon as Little Joe on *Bonanza,* all roguish charm. Or like Gary Cooper in *High Noon,* the strong, silent type.

As Cassie and Jasper walked in, Tyler was inexpertly wiping down the table with a damp paper towel while Adam packed in a sack the small amount of groceries Jasper had stored in the cupboard. Still thinking of Cassie and Kevin Costner, or some other cowboy of the same studly ilk, Adam looked up with a frown on his face. He quickly realized that Cassie had mistaken his gloomy expression as a distaste for baby-sitting.

Her cheerful smile wavering, her gray eyes searching his, she inquired, "Did you two manage okay without us?"

"Sure, Mommy," Tyler answered for them. "We

ate sand'iches and now we're cleanin' up. Can we go now?''

"As soon as we're packed, bud," Jasper told him. "Come on over here and help me unload this drawer."

Tyler did as he was told and Adam and Cassie were left in the relative privacy of the kitchen.

"We had a great time and Tyler's a great kid," Adam immediately told her.

She didn't look convinced. "Then why were you frowning when we came in?"

"I was thinking about Kevin Costner," he replied dryly.

Her eyes narrowed, her lips tilted. "Say again?"

"Look, don't ask. Just believe me when I say I wasn't frowning because of Tyler. He behaved perfectly and we had a couple of great 'sand'iches.'"

Finally she smiled. "Okay, I believe you." She looked like she wanted to say more, to ask questions and find out what he was thinking and feeling, but she didn't. For this he was grateful.

"Did your father give you much trouble?" he asked in a low voice. He eyed Jasper across the room, tossing clothes in suitcases and keeping up a nonstop conversation with an excited Tyler. "He looks a little less bloodthirsty now."

"Don't worry about Dad. He'll warm up to you. It just takes him a while to trust people."

You could take some lessons from him, Cassie, Adam thought, but since it wasn't time for a confession, he kept this opinion to himself.

Soon Jasper and Ty were packed and ready to go. In just a few minutes they were taking off from Lake

Hood with Tyler in the front passenger seat, and Cassie and her father in the rear. Tyler's excitement was palpable, his eyes enormous, his cheeks rosy with color. If he was a little frightened during the takeoff he didn't show it and once in the air he couldn't quit asking questions.

Cassie was sitting behind Adam and she leaned forward to whisper wryly, "Like mother like son."

Adam smiled and nodded. Yep, they were alike all right, equally intelligent and inquisitive, equally engaging. Thank God, though, Tyler proved he wasn't too perfect. Toward the end of the flight, he started getting irritable and bored, then announced that he had to go to the bathroom...*now*.

"Honey, why didn't you go before we left the hotel?" Cassie asked in a beleaguered voice.

"No one tol' me to."

"Some things you shouldn't have to be told, Tyler," his grandfather stated unequivocally. "I'm sure you can wait till we land."

"When will we land?" Tyler wanted to know, his voice grown slightly whiny.

"In about five minutes," Adam said. "We'll land in the water right by my house, Tyler, and all you'll have to do is run up the stairs to the bathroom. Think you can make it?"

Tyler considered, then mumbled, "Yeah, I think so. I'll tell ya if I can't."

"I'd appreciate that," Adam murmured. He caught Cassie's chagrined expression in the overhead mirror and he smiled at her. She was so eager that Ty make a good impression, but she shouldn't be worrying. If Tyler didn't whine or get bored or have to go to the bathroom at the most inconvenient moment, he wouldn't be normal. His normalcy certainly took nothing away from Adam's appreciation of his nephew. Actually it just made him more real and lovable. He wondered if Alex would see it the same way...

As soon as they docked in Seldovia, Cassie accompanied Tyler up the stairs at a brisk trot to the nearest bathroom while Jasper and Adam followed more slowly with the suitcases.

"I've always wanted to see Alaska," Jasper commented as he took in the view. "It doesn't disappoint."

"There's no place like it," Adam agreed, then added politely, "but Montana's nice, too."

"It's home," Jasper said, then turned his gaze on Adam. "For all of us."

Adam suspected a double meaning. Perhaps Jasper was cautioning him about trying to take Tyler away from the only home he'd ever known. Since he had no right to do so even if he wanted to, Adam quickly reassured him. "You have nothing to worry about, Mr. Montgomery."

"I don't?" Jasper had stopped on the stairs and was looking Adam straight in the eye. "Would you care to elaborate on that?"

Adam smiled wanly. "No. Just please believe me when I say I don't want Cassie or Tyler hurt any more than you do."

Jasper stared at Adam for a minute, then sniffed and looked away. "Don't know why, but I think I actually *do* believe you," he said grudgingly.

"Doesn't mean I won't be watchin' you like a hawk, though."

Adam chuckled and started up the stairs again. "Can't say I blame you, sir."

"Adam?"

Adam turned. "Yes?"

"Don't call me sir. Makes me feel like an old fart. Jasper's the name. Use it."

Adam suppressed a smile and nodded soberly, liking Cassie's father more by the minute. At the top of the stairs, Adam directed Jasper to the main cabin and down the hall to one of the two extra bedrooms, passing Cassie and Tyler in the kitchen getting drinks of water. He set down the suitcase he was carrying and said, "Furnishings are kind of spare, but this is the best mattress of the two available."

"All I need is a place to lay my head." Jasper looked around consideringly. "You say you've got two empty beds? How many bedrooms have you got in this house, anyway?"

"Three."

Jasper was immediately on the alert. "Where's Cassie sleepin', then?"

Adam pointed toward the window. "See that little cabin down the hill a ways? Cassie has it all to herself."

Jasper's eyes narrowed. "You put her there right from the start, not just when you heard I was comin'?"

"I'm very happy to say that yes, I put her there right from the start," Adam answered with rueful amusement in his voice. "Very happy, indeed."

This drew a reluctant grin from Jasper. "I'll bet you are."

Adam nodded, the two of them understanding each other perfectly. "So where will Tyler stay, with you or Cassie? Or would he like his own room?"

"He's got his own room back home, but while he's here I expect he'll want to stay with me or his mom. We'll let him choose, but I'll put his clothes in this chest of drawers with mine." He turned toward the door where Cassie and Tyler had just appeared. "That okay with you, hon?"

Cassie shrugged, smiled. "Fine with me. Tyler can sleep where he wants. It's up to him." Cassie looked down at Tyler. "Where do you want to sleep, Ty? Here in the big house with Granddad, or with me in the little house down the hill?"

"I'll sleep with the guys," Tyler answered importantly, strutting into the room and sitting down on the edge of the bed. "Say, when are we goin' to see that eagle's nest you tol' us about, Uncle Adam?"

"As soon as you guys get unpacked and settled in, we'll do some sight-seeing, get a good look at the eagle's nest, then take the ferry over to Halibut Cove for some dinner."

"What about fishin'?"

"We can do that tomorrow morning before the wedding rehearsal. Sound okay?"

Tyler wrinkled his nose. "Who's gettin' married? Do we hafta go to the weddin'?"

"I'll let your mother explain about the wedding," Adam said, exchanging an amused smile with Cassie. "I have to get something in my car."

Adam left and went straight to his car, picked up his cell phone and called his brother's home number. For what he had to say to Alex he needed privacy. The phone rang five times, then went to Alex's answering machine.

"Damn," Adam grumbled. He wanted to talk to Alex and make his position known immediately. He wanted to tell Cassie the truth. The sooner the better. The fact that they'd soon be on honest terms with each other was the only thing that gave him the courage to keep up the charade.

After the beep on Alex's answering machine sounded, Adam said, "Alex, we have to talk. Tonight." He hung up without going into further detail just in case Kelly was around to hear the recorded message. No point in tipping their hand before Alex had time to prepare his fiancée for the startling news.

Adam pressed the Off button on his phone and turned just in time to see Cassie walking slowly down the wooden walkway to her cabin. She didn't glance his way but seemed preoccupied with her own thoughts...apparently happy ones, judging by her serene expression.

Adam shook his head sadly. Too bad he was going to have to burst her bubble soon. But until that dreaded moment, he was going to make sure she and Tyler and Jasper had a wonderful afternoon and evening. For Adam their time together would be bittersweet, because after his and Alex's confession it was highly unlikely that Cassie would ever want to speak to him again.

WITH THE THREE most important men in her life as company, Cassie had never spent a more wonderful afternoon and evening. Adam drove them all over the place. They saw mountains and hanging glaciers and streams and lakes. They got out and took short hikes into the forest and saw moose and caribou and even a black bear. The highlight of the trip, though, was the eagle's nest.

They'd parked in a meadowlike clearing that was covered with glorious purple lupine, the area surrounded by old conifer and cottonwood trees. They stood, four abreast, by the Jeep. Adam handed Cassie and Jasper each a pair of binoculars, then turned to Tyler.

"Here's your pair, kiddo. Are they too heavy for you?"

"No, o' course not," Tyler answered stoutly.

"Good. Now come here and let me hoist you up on my shoulders. Take your hat off first." Adam grabbed Tyler under the arms and lifted him over his head easily. "I'll tell you where to look, okay?"

"Will there be baby eagles in the nest?" Tyler asked as he settled himself on Adam's shoulders.

Adam held Tyler loosely by his ankles. "There should be. Usually the nests are built in April, the eggs are hatched, then by the end of July most of the eaglets are ready to fly. See where I'm pointing?"

"Yeah?"

"Look through the binoculars at that tree, the really tall one in the middle of the three that are clumped close together. Do you know which one I mean?"

"Think so."

"Good. About a third of the way down you'll see the nest. It's pretty big, so—"

"I see it! I see it!" Tyler bounced on Adam's shoulders, accidentally bumping Adam's head with the binoculars.

Adam winced, but didn't mention the unintentional assault. Cassie pressed her fingers against her mouth to stifle a giggle.

"Do you see the eaglets?"

"Yeah! They look funny. All fuzzy and feathery."

Adam chuckled. "Yep, they look pretty funny when they're little. It'll take awhile before they get sleek and beautiful like their mom and dad."

Suddenly they heard an eagle's cry in the sky above them and an adult eagle fluttered gracefully down to perch on the edge of the nest.

"I'll be damned," Jasper muttered. "Ain't that a pretty sight?"

"Yes. The prettiest sight I've ever seen." But Cassie wasn't talking about the mother eagle and her young. She held the binoculars away from her eyes and was gazing at Adam and Tyler, both of their faces rapt and smiling. Her heart ached and a lump of emotion filled her throat. She wished she knew if Tyler and his father would be enjoying more excursions together in the future, but Adam still wasn't giving her any clues.

From the Homer harbor they took a ferry to Halibut Cove, which Adam said was an artists' colony, with about a dozen blocks of wooden walkways that connected galleries, eateries and private homes. They ate at the Saltry where they sat at a window that overlooked the boat dock and the cove. Everyone had seafood, Adam and Cassie enjoying some exotically prepared halibut, Jasper and Tyler sticking with pan-fried fillets of salmon.

Tyler was nodding by the time they headed home, sated with good food, fresh air and breathtaking scenery. Even Cassie, despite the growing yearning she felt for a fairy-tale ending of this incredible trip to Alaska and the almost nonexistent chance of such a thing ever happening, felt contented to the core. She was living in the moment, savoring the day for all it was worth. Who knew when she'd ever be this happy again?

Back in Seldovia, Cassie helped Tyler into his pajamas and into bed, where he fell asleep immediately.

"I'm hittin' the hay, too," Jasper announced as he stifled a yawn. "But I'll walk you down to your cabin first."

"No need, Dad," Cassie assured him.

Jasper peered at her concernedly, obviously struggling to keep his eyes open. "You *are* goin' straight down to the cabin, aren't you?"

"Yes. It's ten-thirty and we're supposed to get up at the crack of dawn to go fishing, aren't we? Dawn comes pretty early up here in the summer, so I think it's best I get some sleep."

Jasper looked past her to the door. "Where's Adam?"

Cassie shook her head, grinned ruefully. "Dad, I told you not to worry. Adam's already said goodnight. He took the car and went into Seldovia to see Alex about something. He said he'd be late."

Jasper nodded. "Good. Then I'll say good-night, too, sweetheart. Sleep tight."

"I will, Dad." She kissed him on the cheek, then stooped to kiss Tyler, too.

"Close the door in case Adam's not so quiet when he comes in," Jasper told her.

She obeyed and was soon on her way down to her own private little retreat. It was still light outside and she looked toward the gravel drive by the house half hoping that Adam's Jeep would pull up while she was watching. She'd been disappointed when he'd announced that he was going to Alex's. She had hoped they could spend a little one-on-one time together at the end of the evening. She was anxious to know how he was thinking, feeling. About Tyler, of course. But also about *them*.

While Jasper was around, there was no possibility of physical contact of any kind, but Cassie had felt the sexual tension between them all day long. Even now, even when Adam was nowhere in sight, she positively *ached* for him. But now it wasn't just physical desire she felt. She wasn't being swept off her feet by a handsome, charming stranger who hadn't even told her his real name before making passionate love to her. This time she was getting to know him, seeing him in his natural surroundings, watching him with their son. If they made love now, it would be different. It would mean something more...

As Cassie prepared for bed, she tried to force visions of their lovemaking out of her mind. By the time she'd showered, brushed her teeth and slipped into her nightie, she realized that she wasn't going to get any sleep at all that night. She was too keyed up. She needed to relax somehow. Then, suddenly, she remembered the hot tub.

ADAM KNEW it was probably fruitless, but he drove past Alex's house one more time. Sure enough, there was no car in the drive, no light on in the house. It wasn't possible his brother was spending the night with Kelly in Kenai because her parents were staying at her apartment, but they could be out on a late date together and he just hadn't received Adam's phone messages yet.

Adam sighed and headed home. At least by now Cassie, her father and Tyler would be in bed and asleep. He wouldn't have to be around Cassie until tomorrow, wouldn't have to fight his ever-growing desire to kiss her, hold her, make love to her. After she learned the truth, she'd probably hightail it back to Montana as fast as she could. Then there'd be no more temptation, no chance of doing something so morally bankrupt as making love to a woman he'd blatantly lied to about something as sacred as the paternity of her child.

Adam was careful to be very quiet when he entered the house. He noticed that Jasper's door was closed and heard loud snoring coming from behind it. He wondered how Tyler managed to sleep through such a ruckus, but then remembered that kids could sleep through just about anything, bless 'em. And troubles didn't keep them up at night, either. They were either too innocent to realize they should be worried, or were too optimistic to think that troubles might actually outlast the night and reappear the following morning.

Adam wished he had a small portion of such innocence and optimism. Enough, at least, to get him through what might be the longest night of his life. That Cassie was sleeping just a few yards away nearly drove him crazy.

He showered, brushed his teeth, pulled on his pajamas, then hit the sack with the latest techno-thriller guaranteed to keep you enthralled until the last chapter. Fat chance. After ten minutes, he threw the book on the lonely-looking pillow next to him, tossed off the covers and tore off his pajamas. Stepping into his swim trunks, he grabbed a towel and headed for the hot tub.

Just feet from the screened-in patio that housed the sunken hot tub, Adam stopped short. In the gloaming of approaching midnight, he could see that the tub was already occupied. It could only be one person, of course—*Cassie*.

Adam's heart began to thump wildly. His breathing accelerated. His skin tingled and anticipated. This was the best and the worst coincidence possible.

If he was smart he'd turn around and head back to the house pronto. But he wasn't feeling smart. He wasn't feeling much of anything beyond a yearning to see, to hear, to *touch* the woman who had been dominating his thoughts since her letter arrived two weeks ago. And every hour in her presence since then had intensified his desire for her.

Slowly Adam moved closer and closer to where the hot tub bubbled away invitingly. But far more inviting than the warm, pulsating water was the idea of sharing it with Cassie. Standing in the shadows of a low-hanging tree branch, he stopped and stared, at war with himself. He knew he shouldn't be spying on her, but he couldn't help himself.

Cassie was up to her collarbone in water, her arms stretched out on either side, the back of her head resting against the molded side of the tub. A smile played on her lips, her eyes were closed. He feasted on the sight of her, the curve of her long throat, that pulsing dip at the base of it, the gentle slope of shoulders, the suggestion just below the frothy waterline of small, firm breasts.

That's when he realized she was naked. That's when he knew he'd better leave. He was no Peeping Tom. He turned to go.

"Adam? Adam, is that you?"

Adam turned back, but looked everywhere except directly at Cassie. At a *naked* Cassie. "Yeah, Cass. It's me. But I'm headed back to the house. I didn't know the tub was occupied."

She chuckled. "It's a big tub, Adam. Why don't you join me?"

He flitted an alarmed look at her—at those big eyes, that glistening skin—then away again. He swallowed hard. "I don't think that would be a good idea."

"Why not? This would be a great time and place for us to talk. We haven't had a private moment all day."

He felt the heat creep up his neck and pool in other more sensitive areas of his body. "Talking's okay. It's the privacy part that worries me, Cass. Maybe if you had some clothes on—"

This time she laughed out loud. "Adam! I do have clothes on. My bathing suit straps have just slipped off my shoulders, that's all. See?"

Nervously he allowed his gaze to shift, then rest on Cassie. She had pulled herself out of the water until she was exposed from the waist up. Sure enough she was wearing a bathing suit, a peach-colored bikini that had appeared flesh-colored under the water. The straps were up again, but the minimal covering of her slim, sexy body accomplished by the bikini wasn't enough to tamp down Adam's growing ardor. On the contrary...

"Look, if you're afraid we'll...we'll get involved, I promise to stay on my side of the tub. I promise not to try to seduce you." She slipped back into the water and smiled coyly. "I promise," she repeated.

That's when Adam started to feel like an idiot. Obviously Cassie wanted some company. *His* company. Obviously, they were both adults and they both knew the unfeasibility of getting involved with each other right now. So, surely with both of them attempting to keep cool heads, despite the hot and steamy environment, surely they'd succeed in doing so. It wasn't as if he were some out-of-control hormone-riddled teenager.

"Sure, why not?" he said at last, with more bravura than he felt. He opened the screen door and advanced to the edge of the tub. Staring down at her and seeing her without the blur of the wire meshing between them was startling. She was so beautiful.

Her skin so creamy pink and white, so shiny with moisture.

Perhaps he'd made a mistake...

"For heaven's sake, Adam, get in," Cassie coaxed. "These waters are not shark-infested."

Adam chuckled nervously. Sharks he could maybe handle. A wet and sexy Cassie was something else.

Adam dropped his towel and stepped into the tub. Going down, he couldn't help but feel that, figuratively as well as literally, he'd soon be up to his neck in hot water.

Chapter Eight

Cassie watched as Adam slowly slid into the water. It was the body she remembered, only better somehow. The calves so sinewy and well-developed, the taut thighs, the narrow hips, the flat stomach, the smooth, hairless chest...

Cassie's brows furrowed. Hairless? She distinctly remembered that Adam had had a light dusting of black, curly hair on his chest five years ago. Her fingers had delighted in the silky feel of it. Was it possible that, during the passage of time, a man could go bald on his chest? Not likely!

Then she realized that he could be waxing it. Lots of men did, although she would never have pegged Adam as the type of guy who would feel the need to tamper with nature. She was curious to know the reasoning behind the cosmetic change, but how did you ask such a question? Maybe it had something to do with being a marine biologist and all that scuba diving he did. In her opinion, either way was fine. Hairy or hairless, he had a fine chest.

Adam leaned back in a corner seat of the hot tub,

the water nearly to the top of his shoulders. He closed his eyes and released a long sigh.

"Feel good?" she inquired with a shaky smile.

"Yep."

"It was a pretty tense day for both of us," she continued, eager to talk if for no other reason than to take her mind off what she really wanted to do. She had another good reason to talk, though. She really did want to know what Adam was thinking and feeling about the most important thing they had in common, their *son*. "It's not surprising we both thought of using the tub."

"Uh-huh."

"I couldn't sleep a wink. I kept thinking about...about—"

Adam opened his eyes. "About who? I mean, about what?"

"You were right the first time. I was thinking about you and—"

"Me?"

"You and Tyler."

He closed his eyes again. "Oh."

She waited, but he offered nothing further on the subject. Growing irritated, she demanded, "Adam, are you going to talk to me about Ty or not?"

"Or not," he answered without opening his eyes. "I'm here to relax, Cassie. I can't relax and talk about serious, life-altering issues."

"Okay, but when *will* you talk to me about Tyler?"

"Tomorrow."

"Really, Adam?"

"Absolutely. After tomorrow, you'll know everything you need to know."

Well, that seemed to settle that. "Then what shall we talk about *now?*" she asked rather anxiously.

"Do we have to talk?"

"I *want* to talk. I mean, if we don't talk…"

Adam opened his eyes a crack, their deep blue a striking contrast to the sooty black of his eyelashes. "Cassie, we've been talking all day. Don't feel the need to entertain me. I think we're beyond that. I know you're conversable."

"That's not why I want to talk."

"Then why?"

"Because it gives me something to do, something to think about besides…besides…" Deciding she'd better shut up, she licked her lips nervously.

Adam's eyes flew open. He sat up, cocked his head to the side, gave his bottom lip a cursory chewing. "Cassandra Montgomery, you *promised.*"

Thrilled and frightened by the abruptly sensual tone of his voice, she sat up straighter. "What? What did I promise?"

"You promised not to try to seduce me."

"I'm…I'm *not.* Look, I'm clear over here." She fluttered her hands over the water, indicating her side of the tub.

"You don't have to *do* something to be seductive," he informed her ruefully. "In your case—at least as far as it applies to *me*—all you have to do is be you."

"Oh." Cassie was pretty sure she'd been complimented, but the details were fuzzy. "I still don't know what I'm doing that's so—" she made a comical Greta Garbo face and stretched the word out in a throaty contralto "—*seductive.*"

He grinned. "For one thing, you're being too damned honest for your own good…as usual. You just now practically told me that *you're* thinking about the same thing *I'm* thinking."

Was it possible to blush when you were already up to your chin in hot, bubbling water? "I did?"

"Cassie…"

"Yes, I guess I did," she confessed.

He nodded knowingly, then his gaze shifted to her lips and stayed there. His grin disappeared. "You're wondering how it would feel if I kissed you."

"But…but I *do* know."

"No, you don't," he stated firmly. "Believe me, Cass, my kissing you now would be totally different than the kisses you remember from that night in Nye, Montana."

After considering her answer for a few nervous seconds, she admitted, "I've been thinking so, too."

"But—things being the way they are—you and I both know it might be best if neither of us found out for sure."

She didn't like the suddenly depressed tone of his voice. "Things being the way they are? You mean unsettled?"

"Yes. Unsettled. Precarious. Dangerous."

"I see," she said soberly. But she didn't see. He still said things that made her think he knew something she didn't. Something that he was afraid to share. Could there be another woman, a *significant* other woman, that he didn't want to tell her about?

He leaned back and sighed again, as if soul-weary, peering at her from under those thick, sexy lashes. "That's why it's really stupid that we're in this hot tub together. We're just tempting fate."

"But I *did* keep my promise, Adam," she reminded him. "I *did* try not to seduce you."

His smile was lazy and rueful. "Thank you for at least trying."

"You're welcome." She paused, bit the inside of her lip. "I have just one last question."

"Yes?"

"Did I succeed in not seducing you...or not?"

That was it. That was the clincher. Adam couldn't stand it anymore. He had to kiss the lips that uttered such inflammatory words with such utter ingenuousness. Whether her innocence was an act or not, he didn't care. The effect was the same.

She watched wide-eyed as he crossed the churning water between them in two floating strides, grasped her shoulders and pulled her against him. A feeling of serenity, of profound relief in the final surrender of will to fate swelled through him like a soothing tidal wave. Her skin felt so soft, so warm and welcoming under his hands. He'd wanted to touch her like this for so long! Then the serenity turned to exhilaration and urgency.

"That was one question too many, Cassie," he explained. "But since you asked, here's your answer." He cupped her face and lowered his head until his lips touched hers. He had meant to be gentle, to bank the fiery desire he felt and keep the kiss as restrained as possible. Foolish man. Stupid idea. The minute his lips connected with Cassie's, he was lost.

And it didn't help that she seemed as eager as he, as curious, as lost...

As the kiss deepened, he pulled her close, relishing the feel of her slim curves against him, exulting in the sweet, heady taste of her. His hands slid over her shoulders, her back, into the dip of her waist. Hesitantly at first, then bolder, Cassie touched him, too, her seeking fingers caressing his back, then moving sensuously upward to sink deeply into his hair.

Desire was drowning out the screams of his conscience. Emotion was overcoming his reason. Nothing, no one had ever felt so right.

Cassie was in heaven. Nothing, no one had ever felt so right. Not even her memories of five years ago could compete with the way she was feeling now, today, in Adam's arms and enjoying his kisses as if for the first time.

It *was* different this time. It was better. She had thought it might be better, but not like *this*. There was an emotional intensity behind the kisses and caresses that took her completely by surprise. They seemed connected on a spiritual as well as a physical plane. Oh, but the physical was good, too. So very, *very* good.

Deep in another kiss, their tongues exploring, seeking, tasting, Cassie brought her hands forward to his waist, then up and over the smooth expanse of his chest. Beneath her sensitized fingertips she could feel every nuance of muscle. She pulled back from his kiss just long enough to murmur against his mouth, "I like your chest smooth like this. At first I wondered why—"

Cassie abruptly broke off when she felt him stiffen. She leaned back and peered into his face. The sun was finally setting and his features were partially hidden in shadows. He didn't look at her but past her, into the quickly darkening forest that surrounded them. "Have I offended you? I wasn't going to mention that I'd noticed the difference, but I just sort of got carried away. I *do* like it."

"Well, I suppose I'm glad you like it," Adam said in a strangely strangled voice. "But why do you feel compelled to compare everything *now* to *then?* Hell, Cassie, I feel like I'm competing with myself! That night in Nye is ancient history. *Ancient history!*"

He released her and turned away, leaving Cassie startled and devastated by his apparent anger.

"Adam, I'm so sorry," she whispered, staring helplessly at his back. "I...I had no idea you felt this way."

Abruptly the stiffness went out of his back and his head fell forward in a defeated pose. "It's not your fault, Cass. It's mine. I should never have allowed this to happen." He turned to throw a weak and wistful smile over his shoulder. "I'm the one who should apologize."

Suddenly cold and shaken to the core, Cassie crossed her arms over her chest. "Instead of apologizing to each other, why don't we dry off and go inside so we can talk?"

"No, Cass," he said tiredly. "No talking until tomorrow. That's when everything that needs to be said will be said. I'm going to bed now and I suggest you do the same. It'll be dark in a matter of minutes.''

Before Cassie could say another word, Adam stepped out of the hot tub. Water streamed down his body, accentuating the musculature of his well-honed physique. Gazing at him Cassie couldn't even remember her name, much less find the words to urge him to stay and have a heart-to-heart. He bent to pick up his towel, gave his torso and legs a few cursory swipes, then opened the screen door and headed up the wooden walkway to the house without ever looking back.

Back in her cabin, Cassie tried in vain to understand what exactly had happened in the hot tub between her and Adam. She felt shocked, betrayed, bereft. One minute they were kissing, the emotion and electricity between them equal forces driving them to the inevitable act of lovemaking. Then, suddenly, after her mention of his smooth chest, he had turned away from her as if she'd forcefully applied her knee to his groin!

She didn't believe he could possibly be so vain that mentioning the chest waxing—or rather alluding to it—was taken as an insult. But he was certainly upset about something related to comparing him *now* with him *then*. But why? She knew she'd never sleep if she didn't demand an immediate explanation.

Quickly throwing on jeans, a T-shirt and a pair of slippers, she tied her hair back in a ponytail, then took a flashlight and headed to the house. She knew he was still up. She could see a light on in one of the back bedrooms and in the kitchen.

The back door was ajar, so she pushed open the screen door and quietly went in. She didn't want to wake up her father or Tyler. She tiptoed into the dimly lit kitchen and saw Adam standing in front of the open refrigerator, his back to her. He was fully dressed in jeans and a blue flannel shirt. She supposed he was anticipating a sleepless night, too.

Filled with yearning, filled with the need to fix things between them, she laid the flashlight on the counter, walked soundlessly up to Adam, slipped her arms around his waist and pressed her cheek against his back.

"Adam, I just couldn't leave things the way they were."

Adam jumped when she touched him, then turned around and gazed down at her with an astonished expression. "Don't look so surprised," she whispered, her hands resting flat against his chest. "I had to know why you shut down on me like that. Something's bothering you and I want you to tell me what it is."

"But—"

She touched her fingers to his lips. "I know you said you didn't want to talk tonight, but I can't wait. We can talk about Tyler tomorrow, but, please, let's talk about us *tonight*."

"But I'm not—"

Cassie silenced him with a kiss. When he didn't immediately respond, she just tried harder. She twined her arms around his neck and gave it everything she had. In fact, she was so busy trying to make *him* respond, it took her a while to notice that *she* wasn't feeling much of anything, either.

"What the hell is going on here?"

Cassie froze at the sound of Adam's angry voice. Her eyes flew open as she stared up and into the apologetic and amused expression of a man she had no business kissing. With abrupt and sickening clarity she realized that she'd mistaken Alex for Adam and was liplocking the wrong twin!

ADAM HAD TO force himself to remain calm. Alex had arrived just moments before and Adam had gone to his bedroom to put on some clothes so that he and his brother could take a walk and have a long talk. But coming into the room and seeing Cassie kissing Alex was like a bad dream come true. Because he knew they'd kissed and more before, the image had intruded from time to time, but he never thought he'd actually see them together in the flesh.

"Adam! I thought…I thought he was *you*," Cassie stammered, then practically jumped away from Alex when she realized she still had her arms around his neck.

"I can believe that," Adam said evenly, "but who did Alex think *you* were? You and Kelly could hardly pass for twins."

"Hey, bro, don't get the wrong idea here," Alex cautioned in a cajoling voice, his hands raised in the classic pose of innocence. "Cass took me completely by surprise."

Adam crossed his arms. "Yes, I noticed you were stunned speechless," he said dryly. "You couldn't even pull yourself together long enough to say the three little words that would have cleared things up immediately."

"Three little words?" Alex repeated with a puzzled frown.

"You know... 'I'm not Adam.'"

Cassie moved toward Adam, her hands clasped, her face devoid of color. "Adam, I can vouch for the fact that Alex was stunned. He just stood there while *I* kissed *him.*"

Adam raised a brow. "So are you saying that if he hadn't been stunned, he *would* have kissed you back?"

"You know that's not what I'm saying," Cassie exclaimed in an incredulous tone. "Adam, I don't understand why you're acting like this. You have no reason to suspect Alex of wanting to behave improperly with me. And you certainly have no reason to think that *I* would want to put the moves on *him.* He and I have no history together and, besides, he's engaged to be married! Not only that, but he's my son's uncle!"

Adam had no reply to this. Cassie's reasoning was based on more falsehoods than truths, but she didn't know that. He had immediately accepted that Cassie had made a mistake, that she had mistook his brother for him, but what about Alex? Had he allowed the kiss—perhaps even welcomed it—because of a lingering curiosity about Cassie and the potent memory of her kisses? Was there still a spark between them?

Now Alex approached him and spoke in a low voice. "Listen, bro, I can tell you're thinking way too hard about what just happened here. Plain and simple, this was a mistake. In case you need reminding, let me tell you again that I'm getting married in less than forty-eight hours to a woman I'm crazy about. I wouldn't do anything to jeopardize that. Adam, you *know* I wouldn't.''

Adam stared into his brother's eyes and knew he was telling the truth. His gaze shifted to Cassie. She looked confused and hurt and angry. He didn't blame her a bit. He'd been behaving like a jackass. His own frustration had spilled over into a ridiculous display of suspicion and jealousy.

Adam released a long sigh. ''I'm sorry, Alex, Cassie. I obviously jumped to the wrong conclusion.''

Relief showed immediately on Alex's face. ''Don't worry about it, bro,'' he said, punching Adam on the arm.

''What about you, Cass?'' Adam inquired with a chagrined half smile. ''You still look upset.''

Although her hands had relaxed and her color was back, her brows were fixed in a frown. ''I don't want to be upset with you. I just want to *understand* you. That's why I came up here looking for you, Adam. I want you to explain why you got so upset when I mentioned—'' she darted a look at Alex, then blushed adorably ''—*you know*...the chest thing.''

Adam quickly moved to her side, cupped her elbow and turned her gently toward the door. ''By some miracle, I think your father and Tyler may still be asleep. But if we talk all night in this room, they're sure to wake up eventually.'' As they passed the counter, Alex picked up the flashlight Cassie had brought with her from the cabin.

Cassie watched what he was doing and set her chin at a stubborn angle. ''How long would it take for a simple explanation, Adam? Besides, aren't you and Alex planning to talk?''

"Yes, but not here." Adam smiled, hoping she'd let it go, but Cassie wasn't about to be placated so easily.

"Can't you and I talk first? I don't think Alex would mind."

"It's late, Cassie. Alex wants to get home so he can be rested for the rehearsal tomorrow. And don't forget, we've got a fishing date with Tyler bright and early. I was just getting ready to leave with Alex when you arrived and sort of…stirred things up."

By now, although she was obviously reluctant, he'd managed to maneuver her out the door and they were headed down the walkway toward her cabin.

"Geez, Adam, getting you to talk is like getting Tyler to eat beets," Cassie said at last. "I have questions—"

"I promise you, Cass, tomorrow I'll answer all your questions. We'll have a long talk and clear everything up."

"Everything?" She sounded unconvinced.

"Everything," he assured her.

At the door of the guest house, she turned and peered up at him. In the moonlight he caught a glimmer of a grudging smile. "I suppose I should be flattered that you were jealous when you saw me with Alex. But, really, Adam, I didn't feel anything when I kissed him. He may *look* like you, but he's not you. He could *never* be you."

She stood on tiptoes and kissed his cheek, then disappeared inside, leaving Adam to ponder the irony of her words. After a few seconds, he shook his head and walked quickly back to the house. Alex was waiting for him and he wasn't going to miss this opportunity to get his twin brother alone for a little mano a mano talk.

Alex was standing on the porch, the door to the house closed behind him. "So she picked up on the chest thing. She's got a good memory, I'll say that for her."

"I suspect it's because she's not been with many men."

Alex shrugged. "Maybe. Here, I brought your jacket. Where to, bro?"

Adam took the jacket and slipped into it while Alex held the flashlight. "Let's just walk down the road a bit."

Alex hopped down from the high porch, stuffed his hands in his jean pockets and led the way. "When I got your message, I figured you needed to unburden yourself again. With such an admiration for absolute truth, you'd make a lousy lawyer. Did the kid get to you or something?"

Adam fell into step beside his brother, the bobbing flashlight illuminating the narrow dirt road in front of them. "Hell yes, he got to me. He's an incredible little boy." He took a quick glance at his brother, but could only make out a dim profile limned by moonlight. "I don't suppose you'd want to spend a little time with him and find out for yourself?"

"Not likely," Alex drawled. "Why would you even suggest it...unless you're getting cold feet again and want to bail out on me?" Alex stopped and turned to stare at Adam. Adam didn't have to see his brother's eyes clearly to know the expression in them was anxious and accusing.

"I'm sorry, Alex, but that's exactly what I want to do," Adam answered firmly. "I can't keep lying to Cassie. It's wrong and it isn't fair."

"It isn't fair to whom?" Alex demanded to know. "Cassie? I don't think so, because it seems to me *she's* perfectly happy with the way things are."

"Too happy," Adam said gruffly. "She'd like me to be involved with Tyler, be a father to him."

"Well, why not?"

"Alex, haven't you got a conscience at all?"

Alex ignored him, adding, "By the looks of things, I think Cassie would like you to be something to *her,* too, Adam."

"I wish it were possible—"

"It *is* possible!" Alex exclaimed, exasperated. "Don't be so damned stubborn and self-righteous! You and I are the only two people in the world who know you're not Tyler's real father. I'm sure as hell not going to tell anyone anything different. Why should you?"

Adam closed his eyes on a weary sigh. "Because it's not the truth," he growled between his teeth.

"Truth can be highly overrated," Alex scoffed. "Sometimes, for certain people in certain situations, fiction over fact can make for a much happier existence. Besides, how much closer to being Tyler's real father could you be? You and I share an almost identical DNA makeup—amounts of chest hair excepting—so if you'd actually fathered Tyler he'd probably be no different than he is now!"

"You have this rationalization thing down to a

science, Alex,'' Adam muttered in grim amazement, edging past his brother to continue their walk.

"Can you blame me, Adam? I'm fighting for my life."

"You're exaggerating."

"Kelly *is* my life. If I lose her—''

"I don't think you'll lose her."

"Can you be sure of that?"

Adam paused, then admitted, "No."

"Well, there's one thing we can both be sure of," Alex said. "Whether you tell Cassie the truth or not, you're going to lose *her*."

The harsh, measured words hit Adam like stones to the heart. Alex was right. He was going to lose Cassie whether he told the truth or not.

"Face the facts, Adam," Alex continued mercilessly. "You're so guilt-ridden about lying to her, you'd never let yourself get fully involved with Cassie. You could be a father to Tyler, a husband to her—if that's what both of you wanted—but you won't let that happen. You won't allow the three of you to be happy, because you're too damned honest and upright!''

"If I were really honest and upright, Alex, I wouldn't be in this damn mess in the first place."

"Regardless of when your overzealous conscience kicked in, bro, it's too late for you and Cassie. If you tell her the truth now, she'll be devastated. She'll never forgive you."

"In other words, little brother, you're saying I'm damned if I do and I'm damned if I don't," he commented bitterly. "So what's the definitive point?"

"The point is, since things don't look too good

either way for you, why not save *my* skin? Why not let me and Kelly be happy? Even if you opt to stay out of their lives, Cassie and Ty would ultimately be happier believing you were his father. If you hit her with the truth now, she'll have a bitter taste in her mouth for the rest of her life about Tyler's side of the family. It seems to me that—just to ease your own conscience—you're willing to put the rest of us through hell!''

Adam listened with growing frustration and anger. His brother certainly had a way with words. *He* certainly wouldn't have had any trouble taking up the practice of law. Alex was making him feel as though he were the most selfish person on earth.

Adam knew it wasn't true. He knew he only wanted to do what was right, but he couldn't completely dismiss Alex's argument that by doing what was conventionally "right" he'd be messing up his one-and-only brother's rosy future and breaking the hearts of Cassie and a lot of other people, too.

Adam wasn't sure he believed that fiction was better than fact in any situation, but sometimes the truth hurt so badly it was hard for people to pick up the pieces and go on. Was he, somewhere deep inside, hoping that if Cassie knew the truth she'd be able to handle it, to pick up the pieces and eventually forgive him so they could have a life together? After telling such a huge and sustained lie about something so personal and important, it would probably take a miracle for her to forgive him...but a miracle seemed to be the only hope Adam had.

If he was hoping for a miracle, did that make him selfish? Or just crazy?

"Adam, what are you going to do?"

Without consciously deciding to, Adam and Alex had turned around and had walked to within a few feet of the house. Alex just stood there, his rigid stance a mix of defiance, deference and desperation, waiting for Adam to say something.

As the seconds passed, then the minutes, Adam's anger and frustration built on itself until he was ready to explode. How could he put his brother, Kelly and Kelly's whole family through the misery Alex was so sure would result from Adam's truthtelling? How could he *not?*

"I know you, Adam. If you had decided to tell her the truth, we wouldn't still be standing out here," Alex finally said. Then, sweetly he added, "How can I ever thank you?"

"Don't bother," Adam growled.

The air between them was fraught with tension and resentment. Alex shifted from foot to foot, gave an uneasy chuckle, then suggested, "Look, if it will make you feel any better, why don't you just haul off and hit me?"

The offer was made in jest. But Adam wasn't in a jesting mood. He pulled back his fist and sent it flying.

Chapter Nine

Cassie lay awake in bed thinking about what had happened between her and Adam that night. She also thought about the different things that had happened during the day—things said, looks given—all of which left her no choice but to conclude that Adam was keeping something from her. And Alex knew what it was.

This secret between them was undoubtedly why Alex had paid a midnight visit to Adam on a night when he would have been better off going to bed early so he could be chipper for rehearsal day activities. It had to be something important, something that was really bugging Adam...and maybe Alex, too.

Cassie wasn't stupid. A little naive and trusting, yes. Inexperienced with the opposite sex, definitely yes. But stupid, no. That's why she had to consider the possibility that her father might have been on to something when he'd wondered how the hell she knew which of the Baranof twins was Tyler's father.

She'd answered him quickly and with confidence. It had never entered her mind not to believe that

Adam was telling the truth about being the man she'd made love with five years ago, the man who had fathered her child. To lie about something like that would be cruel and unforgivable. She felt she knew Adam well enough to know he was incapable of being so duplicitous.

Besides, he'd known that she was a virgin when Tyler was conceived. The only way he'd know such a thing is if he'd actually been there, or if, during the five measly minutes she'd spent in the bathroom after announcing who she was, Alex had filled his brother in on all the intimate details of that night in Nye. What a horrible idea!

Cassie sat up and pounded her pillow, then tried to find a cool, comfortable spot on it. She was getting a headache even considering the possibility of such deceit. She refused to believe it was possible for Adam to have made up his mind in five minutes to tell such a huge lie, then act on it for the past two days without breaking into a cold sweat every time he looked at her, her father, or—in particular—her son.

And how had he picked her letter out of hundreds of others if he didn't remember her from somewhere? She'd said it herself and Adam had agreed, it would have been too coincidental, too predestined, for him to have chosen her without some memory prodding him.

Cassie turned on her side and curled up, hugging the covers in tight fists against her chest. She liked Adam. She liked him a lot. And she knew he liked her, too. She was determined not to jump to conclusions. She would put these horrible ideas out of her head for now. She'd give him the benefit of the doubt, give him a chance to explain himself.

One thing in particular she hoped he could explain was the chest hair discrepancy, because now she remembered how Kelly had stroked Alex's chest at Harold's Tux Towne while enumerating the differences between Alex and Adam. There was no denying the fact that her lover of five years ago had had chest hair. Adam didn't. Did Alex? She supposed she could ask Kelly about it, but how did one bring up such a subject?

Cassie squeezed her eyes shut and willed unconsciousness to take over, to rescue her from thoughts that threatened to ruin every hope of happiness she'd entertained in the past two days...but sleep didn't come for a very long time.

Cassie was awakened that morning at the relatively late hour of eight o'clock by Tyler shouting, "Mommy, get up! We've made ya some eggs and you'd better eat 'em so we can get fishin'."

Cassie sat up, pushed her hair out of her eyes and tried to focus. Tyler was leaning on the end of the bed and her father was standing just inside the door.

"We were going to leave you alone till you woke up on your own," he informed her, peering at her appraisingly from under his bushy brows. "But by the looks of things, you'd probably have slept till noon. Have trouble dozin' off last night, did ya?"

"Yes, I guess the sunshine or something has my internal clock all messed up."

"You should've set the alarm," her father told her.

Setting the alarm had never occurred to Cassie.

She'd had serious doubts about ever getting to sleep at all, much less having trouble waking up.

"Don't worry, guys," Cassie said, flipping off her covers and throwing her feet over the side of the bed. "I'll be ready to go in a flash. Keep the eggs hot, I'll be up to the house in ten minutes or less, I promise."

Tyler left with his grandfather, all smiles, and Cassie was as good as her word. She took a quick shower, pulled on the same jeans and pink T-shirt she'd had on the night before when she'd inadvertently kissed the wrong twin, brushed her hair into a ponytail and applied just a dab of lipstick and mascara. She was sure she wouldn't wow Adam with her glamour, but somehow she didn't think salmon fishing and glamour went together, anyway.

Her stomach was in knots as she walked up to the house and she was wondering how she was ever going to eat and keep down a plate of eggs. And now that her mind was filled with suspicion, how was she going to act natural around Adam? She had decided that she would wait until he decided the time was right to talk. She wasn't going to push things. And maybe she was in no hurry to hear the truth, the whole truth and nothing but the truth...

Adam had a hard time meeting Cassie's eyes as she came through the back door, then had trouble looking away. She smiled at him as if nothing had gone down the night before, as if they hadn't kissed and quarreled and promised to clear things up today. It made him hope that maybe she wouldn't push him to talk.

After last night's debacle with his brother, Adam

wasn't sure how to handle things anymore. He still wanted to tell Cassie the truth, but he wanted Alex's full cooperation. And he was determined not to lose his cool again—with Cassie, as he had in the hot tub, or with Alex, as he had during their talk.

After the fact, he'd felt terrible about giving Alex a shiner, especially since he'd still be wearing it for the wedding. And, although Alex had been surprised that Adam had actually taken him up on his suggestion to belt him one, Alex had pulled himself up off the ground without a whimper or a complaint. He'd simply smiled ruefully and hoped his brother felt better.

Trouble was, nothing short of the truth was going to make Adam feel better. He'd thought about all of Alex's arguments last night in favor of keeping mum. In the clear light of day, they didn't wash. Alex thought he was protecting his happiness with Kelly by lying—he even thought he was protecting Cassie and Tyler's happiness—but the truth always came out eventually. And when that happened, no one would be happy.

"Good morning, Cass," Adam said warmly. "I hope you like scrambled." She looked wonderful, so fresh and girl-next-door.

"Scrambled is great," she answered, sitting down at the table.

"Hurry, Mommy," Tyler said, his hands linked around her elbow as he bounced on his heels. "Eat fast, okay?"

"Tyler, leave your mother to eat in peace," Jasper ordered from the living room where he was thumbing through a fishing equipment catalogue. "Have you got your tackle ready, bud?"

Tyler took off, leaving Cassie and Adam alone in the kitchen. Even this marginal privacy felt awkward after last night. And despite her cheerful front, Adam could tell Cassie was tense. She wasn't eating.

"At least drink your orange juice," he suggested.

She looked up, embarrassed. "I'm just not hungry, I guess."

He smiled. "I understand completely."

Cassie nodded, but said nothing. He was a bit puzzled by her restraint, but was too grateful for it to ask questions. She drank her orange juice and they left for Beluga Point in Kenai. Adam had picked that spot for fishing because in addition to salmon he hoped they'd see some white beluga whales for Tyler.

The weather had been excellent since Cassie's arrival on Thursday, but Adam could see clouds gathering over Grewingk Glacier as they found a good spot to throw out their lines. Tyler proved to be an excellent fisherman and his eyes lit up like stars when he got his first nibble. Adam helped him reel in the salmon and laughed out loud at the expression on Tyler's face when he first caught sight of the enormous fish.

"Wow! Look, Mommy. Look, Granddad. He's a *giant!*"

Adam grinned and lifted the ever-present cowboy hat off Tyler's head to ruffle his hair, meeting Cassie's eyes over the crown. "There's some even bigger ones out there, Ty. But we'll catch only enough for dinner and a couple for the freezer, okay?''

"Spoken like a true marine biologist," Cassie commented approvingly.

Jasper limited his catch to just one so Tyler could fish for more than his share, while Cassie watched and cheered them on.

"I thought you'd fish, too," Adam said. "I brought you a rod."

"I love to fish, especially with Ty and Dad, but this experience is so special for Tyler I'd rather just be an observer. His expressions are so fun to watch."

"I know what you mean," Adam agreed. "I can't wait till he sees a whale."

When Tyler did see a whale, his enthusiasm was exhilarating, so much so that Adam realized he must have grown rather blasé over the years to the wonderful creatures he saw on nearly a daily basis and even had the privilege to study. Maybe it was true that you had to see the world through a child's eyes to really appreciate it. And maybe you had to actually spend time with children to appreciate *them*.

Since he and Alex were the only children in his immediate family, there were no nieces or nephews to bounce on their knees or throw in the air until they squealed. They only saw their smaller cousins at large family gatherings, so their experience with children was quite limited. But Adam had found it surprisingly easy to relate to Tyler, to enjoy his company. Maybe if Alex had the same opportunity to spend time with Tyler, he'd decide that chancing Kelly's displeasure was worth the risk to be a father.

This idea stuck with Adam and he made up his mind to make sure, before Cassie and Tyler went back to Montana, that his brother knew what he was giving up by not acknowledging Tyler as his.

By eleven o'clock it had started to sprinkle, then to rain in earnest. They packed up, had lunch at a diner in Kenai, then headed back to Seldovia to get ready for the rehearsal, which was to take place at three o'clock. Tyler immediately went down for a nap in Jasper's room and Cassie retired to her own little cabin without once showing signs of being impatient for their talk. In fact, she seemed as eager as Adam not to be alone with him.

Adam puzzled over this for some time, but Jasper was in a talkative mood and Adam exerted himself to play host until time to get ready for the rehearsal.

ADAM HAD assured her that the rehearsal was informal, followed by dinner at a family-style restaurant in Soldotna, but Cassie took the event quite seriously. She and Tyler would be meeting Adam's family for the first time. She wanted to make a good impression. She still hadn't been given information to the contrary, so she was stubbornly holding on to the belief that Adam was Tyler's father. Especially after watching the two together that morning, Cassie was convinced that Adam couldn't possibly be lying.

Cassie put on a pale yellow, fitted pantsuit, gold hoop earrings and a matching bracelet. She wore her hair down and applied her makeup carefully. She dressed Tyler in a nice pair of khaki pants and a blue pullover shirt that brought out his beautiful blue

Baranof eyes. Her father wore gray slacks, a white Western-style shirt and a black string tie. With his handlebar mustache, he looked like one of the Statler Brothers.

Ironically, Adam's clothing choices were almost identical to what Tyler was wearing! Khaki pants and a blue pullover brought out Adam's beautiful blue Baranof eyes, too. Seeing him and Ty together took Cassie's breath away. Again she told herself he couldn't possibly have lied about being Ty's father, especially since he was going to be introducing them to his family. He wouldn't lie to his whole family, would he?

It had been raining off and on all afternoon, the showers interspersed with brilliant sunshine. Tyler had counted three rainbows so far. The bright blue sky was filled with streaks of fast-moving clouds when they left for the church, which Adam told her was in the old, original town of Ninilchik, a few miles north of Homer on the beach.

Cassie had seen a few Russian Orthodox churches with their charming architecture and onion domes since her arrival, but she was completely unprepared for the picturesque view that greeted her as they came over the hilltop and down into the tiny village at the mouth of the Ninilchik River.

The church was built of white timber with a steep green roof. Although it was quite small, it had five onion domes topped with crosses. To one side was a graveyard filled with more pristine-white crosses, many of the burial sites enclosed within white picket fences about two feet high.

"This is so charming!" Cassie exclaimed. "I can

certainly see why Alex and Kelly decided to have the ceremony here.''

''At sunset, the view as you look across Cook Inlet can be breathtaking,'' Adam told her.

''Who all's going to be here, son?'' Jasper asked from the back seat.

''The church is quite small, so just the wedding party...which is big enough as it is with Kelly's four sisters as bridesmaids. Their spouses and kids and other immediate family members of the wedding party will meet us at the restaurant for the rehearsal dinner later. You won't meet the whole batch of Baranofs and Armstrongs till tomorrow.'' Adam added wryly, ''That'll be a mob scene.''

''Will there be *some* kids today, Uncle Adam?'' Tyler wanted to know, his voice a bit plaintive.

Adam smiled at Tyler in the rearview mirror. ''There'll be two. Kelly's niece and nephew are flower girl and ring bearer. I think they're just about your age, Tyler.''

Tyler nodded. ''Good.''

Adam parked in front of the building just as another four-wheel-drive pulled into the lot. ''It looks like Mom and Dad are here,'' he announced.

Now the flutterings in Cassie's stomach magnified, felt more like hummingbirds than butterflies. What would they say? What would *she* say? What would they think of her and Ty? Would they blame her for bringing Tyler to Alaska? For being careless enough to get pregnant in the first place?

By the time everyone was out of the cars and lined up on the walkway in front of the church for introductions, Cassie had worked herself into a panic. She was surprised and comforted when Adam slipped his fingers over hers and held her hand tightly. She looked up into his face and realized he was as nervous as she was.

"Mom, Dad, this is Cassandra, her son, Tyler, and her father, Jasper Montgomery. Jasper, Cassie, Ty...my parents, Peter and Monica Baranof."

Adam's father was tall and dark with striking wings of gray over his temples. His mother was tall, too, and—surprisingly—a blonde. They were handsome people both, and Cassie could see where Adam and Alex got their good looks. Neither parent looked much over forty, although they'd have to be even if they'd had the twins at an early age.

"It's nice to meet you," Peter said politely, his brow slightly furrowed, his gaze tense and uneasy as he briefly scanned Cassie and Jasper, then settled with keen interest on Tyler.

"Same here," Jasper returned as he reached out to shake Peter's hand.

The two fathers shook hands, then Tyler extended his hand to Mr. Baranof, too. Adam's father looked surprised but rather pleased and bent to shake Tyler's hand. Neither Cassie nor Monica had spoken yet. Cassie was still drumming up her courage, and Monica was too busy staring at Tyler.

"My goodness, it's uncanny how much he looks like—"

"Er...Mom, did I mention that Ty caught some king salmon this morning?" Adam quickly interrupted. Apparently Alex had told their parents everything but the *tiny* little detail that Tyler didn't know Adam was his father. "Show her how big they were, Tyler."

"*This* big," Tyler said, his eyes wide with remembered awe, his arms stretched as far as they would go. "Uncle Adam helped me reel 'im in."

Monica and Peter stared at Tyler as if entranced. Then, finally, Monica broke away long enough to flit a puzzled and disapproving glance at her son. "*Uncle* Adam helped you?"

"Yeah. We caught four of 'em. Two for dinner and two for the freezer."

Tyler's words were followed by silence. Cassie still hadn't said anything and Adam's parents seemed tongue-tied and incapable of doing anything but staring at their grandson. Tyler was beginning to fidget, so Jasper made a move.

"I think I'll walk Tyler around the grounds," he told them. "I expect you four need a little time to…er…clear the air. Come on, son."

After Jasper walked away with Tyler toward the quaint and beautiful graveyard, Peter and Monica's gaze shifted to Adam. "Why does he call you uncle?" Peter immediately demanded to know.

"It was my idea, Mr. Baranof," Cassie said. "I didn't want Tyler to know Adam was his father until…until certain things were worked out."

Monica and Peter turned their attention to her. As if seeming to finally recognize how uncomfortable Cassie was, Monica smiled and touched her arm. "Please call us by our first names, Cassie. This must be hard for you, dear, and we haven't made it any easier, have we? We haven't exchanged a single civil word! You'll have to forgive us for behaving so strangely. It was such a shock when Alex told us. I mean, to find out you have a grandson who is four years old that you had no idea existed... Then, just when we thought we were getting used to the idea, seeing him in person threw us both for a loop.'' She turned to Peter. "Isn't that right, dear?"

Peter nodded, but looked sternly at Adam. "What I don't understand is why you haven't called and spoken to us directly, Adam. Why did we have to hear everything from Alex?"

"I found out about this the same night you did," Adam answered, his tone a bit defensive. "I've needed time to think."

"Well, if he's still calling you Uncle Adam, it sounds to me like you haven't been thinking nearly enough...or *clearly* enough. Alex told us you were having doubts about what to do. I gather you still haven't decided whether or not to be a father to the boy?" Peter glanced down at Cassie and Adam's locked hands. "What *is* going on, Adam?"

Cassie was feeling more and more uncomfortable. She had thought Adam would have called his parents by now, would have talked the situation over with them, explained that Tyler was unaware of the familial connection between them. That he hadn't done so made Adam appear less committed and more confused and conflicted than ever. But she certainly didn't want Adam in their lives if he had to be coerced and shamed by his parents to do it.

Hurt and discouraged, Cassie said, "Maybe I should leave you and your parents alone to talk, Adam." She pulled her hand free and turned to go.

"Cassie, I'll go with you," Monica said hurriedly. ''Why don't you and I get to know one another a little better before the rest of the wedding party arrives?''

Adam watched Cassie and his mother walk away, his heart heavy. He hadn't handled this very well. He should have called his parents before today and made sure they understood what was going on, saved Cassie this confrontation. But how could he do that when, from hour to hour, *he* wasn't even sure what was going on? Alex had put him in a damnable position... No. *He* had put himself in a damnable position. And Cassie, too.

''Well, Adam, *are* you going to tell me what's going on?'' his father repeated.

Adam was tempted to tell him exactly what was going on. Oh, was he ever tempted! His dad had always been a tremendous support to him, a great confidant in times of trouble. But, no, Adam still wanted Alex's willing cooperation in this coming-clean business. He felt the only way Alex would really learn from this situation was to come to the conclusion himself that truth was more important than any tenuous happiness based on lies. Alex had to be the one to recognize his responsibility in this situation and fess up, or he'd blame Adam for squealing on him for the rest of their lives.

Adam lifted his hands in a helpless gesture. ''Dad, things are still up in the air. I *can't* tell you yet what will happen. And, please, although I'm sure the news will be whispered from ear to ear and everyone will know anyway—thanks to Alex—I'd rather the fact that I'm Tyler's father isn't *publicly* discussed. Tyler mustn't know. It's for his own protection.''

Adam's father didn't try to hide his displeasure. "Adam, I'm disappointed in you. If I were father to that child, I'd claim him immediately and be as much a part of his life as possible. Obviously, Cassie would welcome your involvement...and not, I think, just for the boy's sake. Do you really think you're being fair to her, leading her on this way?"

Adam rubbed his forehead. "Dad, I *care* about Cassie. I care about both of them!"

"Then why doesn't Tyler know who you really are? And why aren't you publicly acknowledging him as your son? As much as he resembles you, even if Alex and the others who know are discreet, everyone will guess the truth, anyway. Aunt Zelda in particular can spot Baranof blood from a block away. She won't be here today, but you'll have to face her tomorrow for sure. *And* all the others. As for Cassie..."

He looked over to where Cassie and Monica were standing several yards away, looking out over the tiny cemetery where Jasper and Tyler were carefully wending their way around the neatly fenced graves. Both smiling, they were deep in conversation. "She seems very sweet, Adam. Too sweet to trifle with."

Adam clenched his jaw. He never imagined it would be so hard to lie to his father, to endure his disappointment and censure. "I told you, Dad, I need time," he repeated wearily.

His father shook his head. "This isn't like you, Adam. I think there's more to this than you're saying. But let me leave this word of wisdom with you, son. Family is more important than anything else. If you really do care about Cassie and Tyler—and if it's the kind of caring that families are built on—don't take too long to figure out what to do.''

Adam nodded, a constriction in his throat making it impossible to speak. His father didn't know the whole story, but even if he did he'd still be disappointed in him. Maybe more so. But he'd said words that rang true, words that fueled Adam's own sense of urgency. *If you really do care, don't take too long to figure out what to do.*

His father squeezed his shoulder and walked away as Kelly's car pulled up with her four sisters inside. He saw two other cars coming down the hill, neither of which were Alex's. He wondered how his brother would explain his black eye.

The way Adam was feeling at that moment, he would have gladly blackened Alex's other eye so he'd have a matched set! He wished more than anything that he could announce to the members of his family attending this rehearsal that he really was Tyler's father. Then repeat the announcement tomorrow at the wedding reception in front of the entire Baranof clan. Hell, he wished he could shout it from the summit of the highest peak of the Chigmit Mountains!

But it wouldn't be true. And it wouldn't be fair to Cassie and Tyler. Tyler must never be told such a lie because when the truth came out—which it inevitably would—Cassie would have to try to explain to her son that it wasn't Adam but Alex who was his father. Talk about confusing a kid. Talk about childhood trauma!

No, it seemed Adam's only recourse was to work

on his brother to come clean of his own free will. But how?

AFTER LISTENING to Adam's defensive exchange with his father, Cassie had been close to tears. But Monica Baranof had changed all that. With a warmth and graciousness Cassie couldn't help but respond to, Monica made her feel right at home.

First she asked Cassie questions about her life in Montana, her job, her pastimes. Then, as Jasper and Tyler rejoined them, she encouraged Tyler to tell her all about his Alaskan adventure. By the way her eyes lit up as he enthused about fishing, whales and the eagle's nest, it was obvious she was as thoroughly smitten by her grandson as Cassie had hoped she'd be. It didn't hurt, of course, that he was the spitting image of her own beloved boys. Tyler responded to her, too, but how could he not when she looked at him with such love in her eyes?

The possibility that Monica might not be part of Tyler's life when this trip was over was a thought that couldn't help but dampen Cassie's happiness, but she hadn't given up hope on Adam finally realizing how important Tyler was to him...and, dare she hope, how important *she* was, too?

Monica took Jasper by the arm as she walked them around the outside of the church, pointing out the historically significant details of the building. She explained that they couldn't go inside because the priest—John, a family friend—hadn't arrived yet to open the doors. And once they were inside, reverence for the religious sanctity of the small building would preclude social chattering. John would guide them through the wedding rehearsal and then they'd leave to do more socializing at the restaurant.

Cassie appreciated Monica's attention to her father. She was sure he was feeling threatened by the sudden introduction of more grandparents in Tyler's life, but was too fair-minded and caring to show it.

She glanced over at Adam right after his father walked away to welcome Kelly and four other women. Their eyes met. Adam's gaze conveyed a sort of sad apology. She supposed he was sorry he hadn't been able to make up his mind yet, hadn't better prepared her and his parents for this meeting. Her heart ached, but she didn't go to him. *He* would have to come to *her*. She wasn't going to even inadvertently put pressure on him, especially here among his family and friends.

Things started getting boisterous as the rest of the wedding party seemed to arrive all at once. Cassie watched from a distance as two young men jumped out of a Jeep with mud-encrusted tires. They had a little boy with them. A gray-haired couple arrived in a rented sedan with a little girl bouncing in her seat belt between them. They smiled but seemed reserved and a little disapproving of the festive exuberance of the young people.

"Those are Kelly's parents," Monica explained.

"But they're so much older than you and Peter!" Cassie exclaimed without thinking.

Monica smiled. "They aren't that much older, but they did have children at a later age than most couples. See all those bridesmaids and the two ushers?"

"Yes?"

"All Kelly's sisters and brothers. Kelly's the youngest."

"Oh." Cassie was amazed. She had no idea Kelly's family was so large. And the children seemed so different from the parents, so talkative and full of life.

"Come with me and I'll introduce you to them, then to the others."

Tyler, always a sociable child, immediately asked his mother's permission to make friends with the girl and boy. She said, "Okay, hon. But don't go out of the churchyard and stay away from any mud. And when the rehearsal begins, you must come inside, sit quietly and be respectful." Only half listening, Tyler nodded eagerly and was off to make friends.

Cassie noticed with pleasure that Adam joined their group en route to meet the Armstrongs. He gave her an encouraging smile. She smiled back, glad he would be there to support her while the introductions were performed.

Halfway there, however, another four-wheel-drive pulled into the parking lot. There were two men inside, Alex and another usher, she supposed. Suddenly she stopped in her tracks and stared. Alex stepped out of the vehicle, smiling sheepishly...and sporting a big black eye!

Chapter Ten

As he moved to the center of the group, Alex's appearance caused a general uproar. There were exclamations, questions and jokes about his eye.

"What a shiner!"

"Trying to match your eye to your tux, Alex?"

"How'd that happen? Run into someone's fist?"

"Kelly's, I bet. You two smoothin' out last minute wrinkles in the prenup?"

Alex laughed and shrugged while Kelly hung on to his arm. "Kelly knows better than to hit me where it shows," he joked, after which Kelly punched him playfully on the shoulder. "The truth is—" his gaze traveled across the few feet that separated him from Adam "—my brother hit me."

Cassie was stunned. Everyone was stunned, including, apparently, Adam. He stood as stiff as a board, meeting his brother's bold gaze with a guarded question in his. Or was that a *hopeful* expression? Cassie couldn't really tell.

"What's going on?" Jasper whispered in her ear.

"I don't know," Cassie whispered back. "I...I

never thought Adam would actually hit Alex over what happened.''

"What do you mean...over what happened?" Jasper asked suspiciously.

"Shhh, Dad."

Adam finally spoke up. "Alex is right. I did hit him in the eye last night."

Both sets of parents exchanged glances. "But why, Adam?" his mother wanted to know.

"Why don't you tell her, Alex?" Adam suggested.

Alex continued to stare at Adam with a sort of belligerent half smile on his lips. Cassie was horrified. It seemed like her innocent mistake last night was about to be broadcast to the world! But why would Adam encourage his brother to embarrass her like this?

Suddenly Alex broke eye contact with Adam, looked around at the tense, expectant group and laughed. "Boy, I sure had you guys going, didn't I? It was an accident! Adam and I were horsing around last night, doing a little fake boxing by moonlight, when his fist accidentally connected with my eye. Take my advice, never box in the dark. We had a good laugh over it, but neither of us thought it would turn this ugly. Did we, Adam?"

"No, I never thought it would turn this ugly," Adam answered in measured tones.

The black eye explained, everyone laughed and continued to socialize. Well, not *everyone*. Cassie was still feeling a little shaken by what she had feared would be an extremely embarrassing way to be introduced to the group, not to mention her certainty that Kelly might get a little upset if she found out about the accidental kiss.

The Armstrongs stared at Alex and looked as if someone had forced them to eat worms, and Adam and Jasper stood on either side of Cassie, silent as tombs.

Suddenly Monica took her arm and Jasper's arm and steered them toward the Armstrongs. "Come on, you two," she whispered. "Kelly's parents can't take their eyes off Alex's black eye. Let's divert them!"

Cassie looked over her shoulder and was relieved to see Adam following them. Monica introduced her and Jasper to the Armstrongs and they did manage to divert the scowling couple from unpleasant thoughts connected with the black eye...possibly thoughts having to do with how they were going to answer the impertinent questions that would be asked when they showed off their daughter's wedding pictures! But now those disapproving gazes were fixed on Cassie.

"Nice to meet you," Cassie said in a determinedly friendly tone.

"Same here," Jasper added, as he reached out to shake Mr. Armstrong's hand.

"Nice to meet you, too," they answered in unison, but Cassie could immediately tell that the Armstrongs had heard all about her and Tyler and didn't approve. Their manner was outwardly polite, but she'd seen that appraising look before. Her assessment was unfortunately confirmed when Mrs. Armstrong asked, "Oh, so you decided that it would be best not to bring the little boy?"

Cassie bristled. Did Mrs. Armstrong mean what she thought she meant? That Tyler was an embarrassment? She probably thought it would be best if all three of the Montgomerys stayed at home!

"I take Tyler everywhere I go, Mrs. Armstrong," she quietly assured her, smiling faintly. She looked around the churchyard, saw Tyler and pointed. "That's him right over there. He's the one who looks *just like Adam.*" She probably shouldn't have, but Cassie couldn't help rubbing it in a little!

But Cassie regretted rubbing it in when Mrs. Armstrong blushed and looked flustered. She probably hadn't meant to be offensive. Cassie didn't want to offend anyone, either, much less Kelly's parents, but when it came to Tyler she never made excuses. A terrible tension hung over their little group.

"Come on, Cassie, Jasper," Monica said, her smile forced. "I have several more people to introduce you to."

"Let me introduce them, Mom," Adam offered.

Monica nodded gratefully, looking as embarrassed by Mrs. Armstrong's comment as if she'd made it herself. Adam took Cassie's elbow and guided her into the center of the group. Jasper followed. Adam smoothly introduced them both, then announced proudly, "And I'm sure you know who that little guy over there is...the one who looks just like me?"

Now it was Cassie's turn to be flustered...but in a *good* way! A *very* good way! Adam had seemed passively supportive before, but now he was taking control and actually behaving as though he were proud of Tyler and wanted the whole world to know!

"I see John's coming," Adam said, lifting his chin in the direction of another car coming down the hill. He turned to Alex. "Before he arrives and gets the rehearsal underway, would you and Kelly like to meet Tyler?"

Cassie thought Alex hesitated, but then he casually answered, "Sure. Why not? It's about time I met the nephew I've been hearing so much about."

"I'd love to meet him, too," Kelly assured them. "It looks like he's already made friends with my other niece and nephew."

Now Cassie was sure Adam was coming around to this fatherhood thing! He certainly seemed determined to introduce Tyler to his Uncle Alex. She threw Jasper an encouraged smile as she walked away with Adam, Alex and Kelly. She was disappointed when he did not return the smile, but instead looked rather grim.

When they reached Tyler, he was demonstrating the best way to throw a lasso. "If I hadda rope, it'd be a lot easier," he was explaining to the little boy and girl sitting cross-legged on a dry patch of sidewalk and watching him raptly.

"Ty?"

Tyler turned and looked up at Cassie. "Yeah, Mom? Is it time for the dumb ol' weddin' rehearsal already?"

Cassie smiled apologetically at Kelly. "Just about."

"But we were havin' fun!"

"Watch how you talk about the wedding, sweetheart. We've brought the bride and the groom over to meet you.''

"Oh," Tyler said quietly. Chagrined, he looked up shyly at Alex and Kelly. Adam was standing right next to Alex and it abruptly occurred to Cassie that Tyler had never seen them together before or even knew that Adam had a twin.

His eyes widened with interest. "I can tell you're brothers," he stated. "I can tell 'cause you look a lot alike."

Cassie laughed. "They're not just brothers, Ty. They're twins. They look *exactly* alike."

Tyler cocked his head to the side. "No, Mommy. Not ec'zactly alike. One of 'em's got a black eye."

Everyone laughed. "You're right, but Alex hasn't always got a black eye, Tyler. When his eye looks normal, there's really no way to tell them apart."

"*I* can tell them apart," Tyler insisted. "Even without the black eye."

Cassie knew Tyler wasn't just bragging and she was impressed by her son's perception. She looked at Adam and Alex and still saw absolutely nothing physical about them that was different enough to be able to tell them apart. But there definitely was a difference in their expressions as they looked down at Tyler.

It was strange, but Alex seemed anxious and impatient. Perhaps because he knew the priest had arrived, he was eager to get on with the rehearsal. Or maybe he just wasn't used to children and didn't know what was expected of him.

Adam, on the other hand, had a gleam in his eye that clearly revealed an affection for Tyler. To Cassie it was just further proof that Adam was Ty's father, not Alex.

"You're right, Ty. This is my brother, Alex," Adam said, leaning down and resting his hands on his bent knees so he could be eye-level with Tyler. "He's the lucky guy getting married to that pretty lady over there." He hooked a thumb over his shoulder. "Her name is Kelly. Why don't you shake hands?"

Adam watched while Tyler reached up and Alex reached down. He knew he was forcing this meeting, this contact between them. But, if left to his own devices, Alex would probably have avoided Tyler completely.

"Pleased t' meet cha," Tyler said, shaking hands in a very manly way.

"Pleased to meet you," Alex answered rather faintly.

"Oh, Alex, isn't he adorable?" Kelly cooed.

Tyler frowned at the sissified adjective being applied to him and snatched a glance over his shoulder at his little friends to make sure they weren't laughing. Adam couldn't believe Kelly was talking about Tyler as if he weren't even there.

"Those eyes, that *chin!* Alex, it's just like your—"

"So, I hear you went fishing today, Tyler," Alex interrupted as he gave Kelly a gentle elbow in the ribs.

"Yeah. Me and Uncle Adam caught some really big salmon." His head cocked to the side, his brows drawn together in concentration. "Say, if he's my uncle, are you my uncle, too?"

Adam watched Alex's reaction. He wondered if he would be able to tell Tyler to his face that he was his *uncle*. At least Adam had had the advantage of actually being his uncle. There was an instant of painful confusion in Alex's expression, but then he quickly answered, "Sure, Tyler. Call me uncle. I like the sound of that."

Adam was disappointed. Alex seemed to have put up an impenetrable barrier, making certain that Tyler would have no effect on him at all. He was single-minded in his goal to get married without making any earth-shattering—or *engagement-endangering*—confessions.

Alex turned to Kelly with a smile. "I think it's time we got this show on the road, don't you, hon? I see John's opened the doors to the church and our parents are waiting for us."

"Kelly, why don't you and Cassie and the kids go on in?" Adam said pleasantly. "I need to speak with Alex for just a minute."

Kelly chuckled. "Okay. But try to control yourself, Adam. Don't blacken his other eye, too!"

Cassie left, but threw a questioning look over her shoulder as she urged Tyler ahead with a hand resting on his neck. As soon as the women were out of earshot, Adam turned his back to the church, crossed his arms, and faced Alex. "What was that little show you put on when you first got here?" he inquired grimly.

"What show?" Alex muttered.

"You know exactly what I mean."

Alex shrugged. "Oh, you mean telling them that

you'd hit me? I suppose you thought I'd tell them I'd walked into a tree or some dumb thing.''

"I certainly never expected you to tell the truth, but I wish—"

"You wish I hadn't scared you like that? Well, Adam, you're so keen on telling the truth all the time and I just thought I'd give you an idea—just the *tiniest* taste, of course—of what it would be like to tell Kelly, Cassie and our families the truth about who Tyler's real father is.''

"Alex, I wasn't going to say I wish you hadn't scared me. I was hoping like hell you'd spill your guts, tell it all! I was praying you'd finally realized that there was no other choice but to tell the truth. I was so disappointed when you backed down and resorted to that stupid boxing story.''

Alex sneered. "I don't believe you.''

"Believe me. No matter how much trouble it causes initially, you know you have to tell Kelly, and I have to tell Cassie, exactly what we've done. We have to tell the truth. You *know* it, Alex.''

Alex shook his head. "No, I don't know it. And what about you and *your* little tricks? What's the idea of dragging us over here to meet Tyler? Meeting him doesn't make any difference in the way I feel. He's a nice kid, but so what? You're wasting your time and your breath, bro. Give it up.'' He looked over Adam's shoulder at the church. "Now, if you don't mind, it's not polite to leave a bride waiting at the altar.''

As Alex walked past, Adam caught his arm and growled, "Fine, little brother, but think about what you'll be saying tomorrow when you take your vows for real. Think about what it means to be the person Kelly will promise to love and honor for the rest of her life, and what it means to love and honor her back. Think about it, Alex.''

CASSIE HAD NEVER before attended a marriage ceremony in a Russian Orthodox church, or anything like it. While this was simply a rehearsal, she was still deeply moved. The priest explained each of the steps in the ceremony, its meaning and importance, then actually walked them through some of it.

The couple exchanged rings right at the beginning, then held hands throughout the rest of the service. The theme that stood out most to Cassie was the idea that as husband and wife they'd share everything, joys as well as sorrows. That they would bear one another's burdens.

Watching Alex's and Kelly's profiles from her seat on the far left in the front, she thought Kelly glowed. Alex, on the other hand, seemed wooden and preoccupied. Not *pleasantly* preoccupied, either. She caught Adam's eye once during the rehearsal and his smile was bleak. This was supposed to be a joyous event, but the brothers Baranof didn't look very happy.

When Adam had sent them ahead into the church so he could have a private moment with Alex, she couldn't help but wonder if they were exchanging angry words over last night's accidental kiss. And how about Alex's black eye? Was that really an accident, too?

Cassie knew she couldn't ignore the tension between the brothers anymore and blind herself to clues that pointed in a direction she couldn't bear thinking about. She had to find out what was going on between Adam and Alex and if it had anything to do with a summer's night five years ago in Nye, Montana. She had to ask Adam questions and demand answers. She had to know the truth, no matter how much it might hurt.

She sighed and it must have been louder than she thought. Her dad's arm crept around her shoulder and she looked up into sympathetic eyes. "Don't worry, Cass," he whispered, almost as if he'd read her mind. "We're gonna sort this out...*real soon.*"

SOMEHOW CASSIE made it through the rehearsal dinner. Tyler had fun with the children and Cassie enjoyed meeting more of Adam's family, all of whom treated her with friendly, congenial attention, but underneath it all, she felt a stomach-churning tension. There was never a private opportunity to speak to Adam alone, so she had no choice but to wait until they got home before unburdening her heart and mind of so many emotions and questions.

Adam and Alex kept a healthy distance between them the whole time. And when toasts were made to the happy couple, Adam's was conspicuously absent. When finally asked why the best man wasn't proposing a toast, Adam answered, "I'm saving mine for tomorrow."

It poured rain on the way home. Everyone in the Jeep was quiet and Tyler fell asleep en route, not even stirring during the ferry ride. He was happily exhausted from hours of playing with Kelly's nieces and nephews. Cassie tucked him in bed as soon as they got home, then eagerly went back to the living room to find Adam and demand to know what was going on between him and Alex and what it had to do with her. But when she got there, she found only her father waiting for her.

"Dad, where's Adam?"

"He's down at your cabin, waiting for you."

Cassie bit her lip. "So, he knows I want to talk?"

"Looks that way."

Cassie started toward the door, but Jasper stopped her with a light touch on the shoulder. "Cass?"

Cassie turned. "Yes, Dad?"

"Before you go, I just want you to know that while I've kept my mouth shut for a spell now, I've been keepin' my eyes and my mind open. If you're still confused after talking to Adam, you talk to me. I have some pretty good ideas about what's going on here, but I think it's best Adam tells you first." Cassie nodded. Her father sounded so serious and certain. That wasn't a good sign. Suppose it was true that Adam wasn't Ty's father? Suppose—

"Get goin', Cass. The sooner the better," her father advised.

Cassie nodded again, her stomach a labyrinth of knots. She stepped out onto the porch and closed the door behind her. The rain drummed on the roof like thunder. There were two umbrellas leaning against the outside wall of the house, but, on an impulse, she ignored them and ran down the path to the cabin without any protection from the downpour.

The shock of cold rain against her skin felt wonderful! It cleared her mind, sharpened her determination to face whatever possible unpleasantness lay before her. But she still hadn't given up hope that there was a logical explanation for the animosity between Adam and Alex, for the conflicting messages she got from Adam about his feelings for her and Tyler, and for the "chest thing."

She reached the cabin, went in and stood dripping on the hardwood floor by the door. Adam was standing in the kitchen, but turned when he heard her enter. His eyes narrowed with consternation.

"Cassie, what were you thinking coming down here without protecting yourself from the rain?" He hurried to the bathroom and came out with a towel. "That rain is damned cold. You'll get sick!" He held the towel out to her.

Cassie said nothing, did nothing, just stood with her arms crossed over her chest like a naughty, humbled child. She was starting to feel the chill, but Adam's concern seemed so real, so wonderful! If she got sick, maybe it would be worth it just to have seen Adam a little frightened, to have enjoyed him being a bit of a fussbudget for her sake. He stood over her, scowling like a thundercloud, and she couldn't help but smile up at him.

She watched him melt, relent, then finally smile back at her. "You're an idiot," he said tenderly, then started to blot the rain off her face with the towel, his ministrations as gentle as a lover's.

Cassie hadn't had seduction on her mind when she left the big house, but now she did. How could this man be so gentle and caring and be the remorseless liar he'd have to be if her and her father's suspicions were true? How could she feel this way about him if he wasn't the wonderful man he seemed to be?

Maybe if he held her... Maybe feeling warm and safe in his arms was the cure for all her doubts and fears. Maybe if he made love to her again, as he had in Nye, she'd recognize her lover from all those years ago. Maybe...

ADAM WAS ENCHANTED. He had asked Jasper to send Cassie down to the cabin so they could talk. But looking down at her now, at the glistening rain on her soft skin, the wet shine on her coyly curved lips, the shivering pose, the loving and hopeful expression in her eyes, all he wanted to do was take care of her. Protect her. Warm her up...one way or the other.

He knew which way he'd *like* to warm her up...but he also knew which way he *should* warm her up. Steeling himself against her sweet allure, he ordered, "Get in the bathroom right away, Cass. Rub yourself down with a towel, dry your hair and change into something warm. I'll have a hot cup of tea waiting for you when you get out."

Cassie seemed simply amused by his sternness, and she didn't budge an inch. He knew she must be freezing because he could see the goose bumps on her arms.

Exasperated, he asked, "Cassie, what's wrong with you? Do you want to get sick?"

She rolled a shoulder. "Will you take care of me if I do?"

Adam swallowed. He had certainly not expected this blatant flirtatiousness from Cassie, especially now when they had important things to discuss. But he liked it...*a lot*...and it was wreaking havoc with his good intentions. He had asked her to meet him here so he could apologize for the tactlessness and narrow-minded behavior of the Armstrongs. So he could explain why he'd been so wishy-washy about everything. So he could tell her the *truth*. He couldn't wait for Alex forever. He didn't even seem to know his brother anymore.

"Cassie, I asked you here so we could talk. We can't talk till you've warmed up. Why are you being so difficult?"

She rolled that sexy shoulder again. Hell, where had she learned to do that? "I'll change if you'll help me undress. My fingers are numb with cold. I don't think I can manage the buttons."

Adam raised a dubious brow. "They are? Let me see." He reached out and took her hands in his. She was right! Her fingers were like ice cubes! If she was already this cold, there was no time to lose.

"I don't know why you're doing this, Cass, but it's not going to work," he informed her. She looked up at him, demure and unrepentant. She was adorable with wet, straggling hair in her eyes, a come-hither pout to her lower lip.

"We're *not* going to make love, because we have to talk, do you hear?" he continued to bluster like a frustrated schoolteacher. She said nothing, but her teeth were starting to chatter and that was the last straw. He bent and swooped her into his arms. She gave a little surprised squeal, then twined her arms around his neck. "I'll help you undress, but that's all. That's *all*, Cass!"

Adam carried her into the bathroom, feeling her slim body shivering against him. He realized only a hot bath was going to warm her up. He set his jaw with grim determination. Somehow he was going to get through this without making love to her.

Adam set her feet on the bathroom floor, reached down to remove her shoes and thin cotton socks while she braced her hands on his shoulders to keep steady. He straightened up, then barked like a drill sergeant, "All right. Take off your clothes."

"I...I t-told y-you, Adam, my f-fingers are t-too cold."

He believed her. She was shaking all over. Quickly he unbuttoned the top of her pantsuit, embarrassed to observe his own warm fingers almost as shaky as hers. He peeled off the wet top and tried not to notice the pretty lace bra she was wearing, especially since the rain had soaked through and rendered it virtually transparent. Rosy, erect nipples showed through the delicate netting.

"Turn around," he ordered, his voice gruff and almost angry.

"D-don't be such a b-bear," she complained, wrinkling her nose at him before turning around. "I d-didn't d-do this on p-purpose."

"That's the damnedest thing about you, Cassie," Adam said ruefully. "You don't plan to be sexy as hell. It just happens naturally."

"Th-thank you, I th-think," she stuttered.

"Don't thank me, just try to stand still."

He unsnapped her bra, slipped the flimsy straps over her creamy shoulders, then the insubstantial scrap of lace fell to the bathroom floor. She started to turn around. He held her still with firm hands on her upper arms. "No. Stay facing that direction, if you don't mind."

She turned her head and smiled back at him. "W-what if I d-didn't plan the seduction, b-but now I w-want it, n-need it, m-more than anything?"

"What you need and ought to want more than anything, young lady, is a hot bath," Adam informed her, trying to ignore the way her words had fanned the hot flame of desire already burning in every molecule of his body. "Now let's...er...get those pants off."

There was a zipper on the side of Cassie's slacks. He unzipped it, then hooked his thumbs in the waistband. As the wet slacks slid over her shapely hips, a pair of white bikini panties was revealed. Swallowing hard, he shut his eyes until the slacks were on the floor, then she leaned on his shoulder with one hand and pulled them over her feet.

"You can leave your panties on. Now stand to the side while I turn on the water." Adam continued to avert his eyes from the beautiful, shivering, almost naked woman who stood not twelve inches away from him as he turned the water on full bore and adjusted its temperature.

Maybe this was part of the payback he deserved for lying to her, he mused as sweat collected on his upper lip. Having her so close, so willing, and so unattainable... Well, he deserved to suffer. But if he'd had a choice, he would have rather had hot bamboo shoots shoved under his fingernails than *this*.

"It's just right now, so step in. Be careful. Don't slip."

"W-what about b-bubbles?"

Adam laughed and looked up at her, inadvertently glimpsing lovely pale globes and pink, puckered nipples behind her loosely crossed arms. He looked away, but not before the rest of her slim curves had made an impression on his already hysterical hormones.

"Just get in, Cass."

He waited, but she didn't move, so he heaved a beleaguered sigh and stood up. "I'll look in the cupboard, but since I'm a bachelor, I can pretty well guarantee—"

Whoops. There it was, a big bottle of vanilla-bean-and-gardenia bubble bath. Now he remembered dimly a weekend with a pretty brunette from Sitka and her penchant for frequent soaks in scented suds.

"Y-you found s-some, d-didn't you?"

"Yes," he answered tersely. "And I'll only let you use it if you don't ask me where it came from. Now get in the tub, Cassie, before I throw you in!"

This time she obeyed. Not a little relieved to finally have his hypothermia patient in hot water—not to mention a foreseeable end to this session of torture he was enduring!—he waited until she was sitting down, then stood over the tub and stared at the wall as he poured the bubble bath somewhere, he hoped, near the running water.

"Hey! You're sp-splashing it all over the place!" Cassie exclaimed, laughing. "G-get closer, Adam. I d-don't bite!"

"That's what you said in the hot tub," he muttered, setting down the bottle of bubble bath on the vanity counter.

"I didn't b-bite you, did I?"

He wouldn't have minded it she had...

"C-come on down to my level, Adam. It's the only w-way you can swoosh w-warm w-water over my back. I'm still s-so c-cold!"

She did still sound cold. "Well, I'll swoosh your back with water, but then I'm leaving. But before I start swooshing, I want you to splash the water around and make lots of bubbles. It'll...er...provide a little camouflage for your...er...self." *And some much needed peace of mind for me!*

She chortled like a child, gleefully enjoying his agony. "All right, I'm splashing. There! Is that g-good enough?"

Adam took a cautious look. She was smiling up at him through a veritable bonanza of bubbles. The water was still pouring into the tub and Cassie was nearly up to her chin in big, round, shiny bubbles. Foamy white suds dotted her face, stuck to her hair and the end of her nose, and even floated in the air around her. She looked adorable...and more desirable than ever.

"Maybe I overdid the bubble bath," he said wryly.

"Well, it certainly covers me up. Isn't that what you wanted?"

"You don't sound cold anymore," he hedged. "Are you sure you still need your back swooshed?"

She immediately started chattering her teeth. "Faker," he accused, but he got down on his knees anyway, turned off the tap, picked up a big blue sponge and started squeezing hot water over her back.

"Oh, Adam, that feels sooo good," she crooned,

her eyes closed, her eyelashes fat and spiky against her pink cheeks. "Don't stop. Please don't stop!"

"You sound like one of those organic shampoo commercials," he teased weakly. *Or my favorite dream about you.*

"Just don't stop," she repeated in a husky voice.

Adam didn't want to stop, but pretty soon he'd have to. He quit squeezing the water over her back and started moving the sponge up and down her supple skin, admiring the curve of her backbone, the graceful dip of her slim waist.

It was plenty hot and steamy in the bathroom, but Adam knew his rising temperature had more to do with his occupation than his location. And if he didn't get out of there pretty soon—

Suddenly she opened her eyes and turned to look at him. Her face was only a couple of inches away. Her mouth kissably close.

"Come on, Adam. I know you want to kiss me. So why don't you already?"

He shook his head firmly. "No, Cass. We have to talk."

She stuck out her bubble-dappled chin. "If you don't kiss me, I'll have to take matters into my own hands."

He paused to wonder what she meant, to consider what to do, to say…an instant too long. She laughed and grabbed his shirtfront with surprisingly strong foam-covered fingers. There was a brief struggle, after which Adam found himself dragged over the rim of the rub and into the bubble bath with Cassie.

Chapter Eleven

"Cassie, *what're you doing?*"

Water lapped over the side of the tub and onto the floor as Adam struggled to sit up. There was obviously way too much water in the tub for two bodies. And way too much temptation...

She slid into a position behind him, wrapped her legs around his waist and her arms around his chest. "I should think it's perfectly obvious what I'm doing, Adam. I'm simply trying to warm myself up by borrowing a little of your body heat."

Well, he had plenty to share.

He tried to gently pry her arms from around his chest. The feel of her warm, firm breasts against his back, even through the thin material of his shirt, was too delectable for words. She was stealing his breath away. She was stealing his will to resist.

"That's a bunch of hooey," he argued halfheartedly. "You're as warm as toast by now."

"Oh, you have no idea," she murmured against his ear, then kissed and nuzzled his neck.

"Oh, I think I do," he answered in a rasp. "But this bath business is risky stuff. If you've ever bathed with a man before, you know it can lead to…to *more,* Cass, and I don't think we're…we're ready to—"

"You know, I've never taken a bath with another person. Certainly not someone of the opposite sex," she mused, her breath against his ear sending chills up and down his spine. "In fact, you're the only man I've ever slept with."

This confession stunned Adam. He knew she'd been a virgin when Alex slept with her, but she hadn't slept with another man since then? Obviously, this was not a woman who gave herself easily. It was a humbling thought. She'd struck him as being inexperienced, but he'd never have guessed just how inexperienced she really was! But for one with so little practice at the art of seduction, she definitely had a natural instinct.

"Adam? Have I surprised you?"

"You never fail to, Cassie."

Her hands roamed up and down his chest, then her fingers—no longer too cold to function, but working at their dexterous best—began to undo his shirt buttons.

"Cassie, before you get me too excited to think straight—"

"You mean you aren't there yet?" she whispered provocatively, her warm mouth working its way down his neck and across his shoulder as his shirt gaped open. Eventually she had all the buttons undone, his shirt off and tossed onto the flooded bathroom floor. Now her fingers massaged his bare chest.

Adam's eyes fluttered shut. His head fell back and

Cassie slid around him, kissing his neck the whole time, until she straddled his waist from the front. Her wet, bare breasts were pressed against his chest now, the hard nipples teasing him to the point of insanity. Soon he would have to touch her.

He opened his eyes and swallowed hard. "You're so beautiful...and so damned determined," he whispered, looking at her flushed face, her sultry, half-closed eyes.

"When something's right, I am," she said. "And tonight I'm determined that you and I are going to make love. Wanna bet against me, Baranof?"

"I'd be crazy to."

He was licked. He knew there was no turning back now. He wanted her so badly every part of him strained to be near her, every nerve tingled with the thrill of her proximity. With a sigh of surrender, a silent prayer that she'd forgive him when she knew the truth, he pulled her to him with a roughness born of desperate need and what felt like a lifetime of denial.

His mouth found hers, hard, eager, demanding. She kissed him back with the same intensity, their bodies arching into each other, their hands curious, seeking, pleasuring.

They parted for air and he ran his hands up her arms, then held her away from him, just so he could look at her, really look at *her* for the first time. Her breasts were so beautiful, so perfectly shaped and weighted to fit in a man's hand. He reached out and cupped them both, then found he'd been right. Cassie's breasts had been made for a man's hands...but not just any man's. *His* hands. A surge of almost painful possessiveness washed over him.

He bent his head and, in turn, took each rosy nipple in his mouth and suckled. She moaned and threaded her fingers in his hair, clutching him to her, arching against his mouth. Her response incited him to a higher and higher state of arousal, of yearning, of soul-deep need.

"We're getting out of this tub," he whispered hoarsely.

Her face crumpled. "No." The word came out a barely audible plea.

He smiled. "And onto the bed."

She smiled and nodded, her lips parted, her breath a thin whistle of air.

He stood up and nearly fell, the bottom of the tub was so slick with bubble bath. Holding on to the towel bar, he managed to step out and onto the floor where a rug floated in the flood waters.

"You should take off your slacks in here," Cassie advised, her eyes wide and full of wonder as she stared at him. "That way, you won't drip as much water through the rest of the house."

He nodded and stared back at her as she rose from the water, naked except for a transparent strip of panties. Oh, she was so beautiful....

HE WAS so beautiful.... Cassie just stood and watched as Adam unzipped his pants and pulled them down, then kicked them off along with his Jockey shorts. Fully aroused, he was the most beautiful specimen of male she'd ever seen. Well, he was the *only* specimen of male she'd ever seen, but she knew he had to be above average in oh-so-many ways.

"Now it's your turn," he said, meaning her panties should come off, too, she supposed. She willingly complied and they stared at each other for another minute or two before he finally reached out and helped her step over the tub. They walked carefully out of the bathroom, grabbing a couple of towels as they went, then rubbed each other down—in between kisses—before falling onto the bed.

By some unspoken mutual agreement they left the lights on. They wanted to see each other, to look into each other's eyes. They wanted to go slow…but they couldn't. Kisses and caresses moved quickly to the need for an ultimate joining.

With his forearms braced on either side of her, his body covering hers, he gazed down at her with a look in his sky-blue eyes that was both joyful and sad. "Cassie, I want you to know I've never wanted to hurt you. I hope you believe me. I hope we can work this—"

She reached up and pressed her fingers gently against his lips. "Just love me, Adam. Love me now and we'll talk later." She moved her hips impatiently under his, connecting with that most intimate part of him. He closed his eyes and a tremor went through him from head to toe. Cassie could see, feel, sense, that he was as deeply affected by her as she was by him. Her power over him was exhilarating, humbling. *Wonderful.* His power over her was welcome and real.

He entered her. They moved together with a passion and tenderness that Cassie had never experienced before. *Never* experienced before…. Not with this man, not with any man. And when they reached their climaxes, even as their bodies were racked with wave after wave of ecstasy, their souls seemed to meet, kiss and converge…for the first time.

That's when Cassie knew Adam had been lying to her all along.

He was not her lover of five years ago. Not Tyler's father. That singular honor belonged to the other Baranof twin…Alex.

From her new perspective, Cassie also realized for the first time that she and Alex had been physically attracted to each other and swept away by a fleeting infatuation, and nothing more. And she knew that now only because she had connected with Adam on a much deeper level. Unfortunately, Adam's lies had made their lovemaking a bittersweet travesty.

Stunned and deeply hurt, Cassie pulled away and turned her back to him when Adam tried to hold her.

"Cassie? Are you all right?"

"Just sleepy," she murmured, too confused and full of pain and anger at that moment to confront him with the truth. She needed to think and she couldn't do that with him holding her.

"Okay, so now I know you don't like to cuddle after lovemaking," he teased, then kissed her shoulder and scooted minimally away…not nearly far enough to allow her to capably sort through her myriad emotions.

As they lay in the afterglow of lovemaking, Cassie felt as though she'd turned to stone. Pretending to be falling asleep, she slowly, ever-so-gently, inched farther away from Adam. Away from the magic of his touch, his heat, she could think. She could decide how to get away before the wedding without causing too big a ruckus. It would kill her to stay.

The Baranof twins had lied long enough and hard enough to ensure her silence. She would accommodate them and leave tomorrow, never to return. Tyler didn't need a father and she certainly didn't need a charming liar in her life.

As the minutes ticked by, the silence of the room punctuated only by Adam's soft breathing, Cassie felt the full tragedy sweep over her. Silently she cried, wiping each tear carefully away with the edge of the sheet. He would never know how much he'd hurt her. How much she'd loved him.

Now HE'D DONE IT. He'd done exactly what he'd promised himself he wouldn't do. He'd made love to Cassie before she knew the truth! But then maybe he'd done so because he knew once the truth was out there was a snowball's chance in hell of her giving him the time of day, much less her body and soul.

Yes, that was her soul he'd melded with during the most sublime moments of their mating. He loved this woman—yes, he *loved* her—and they seemed to be meant for each other. If only...

Adam shifted carefully in the bed and peered over Cassie's shoulder to look at her face. She didn't move. Her eyes were still closed. How he wished his mind was as untroubled, then maybe he'd be able to sleep, too.

Oh, if only he hadn't lied to her! If only he'd told her the truth long before tonight, instead of waiting for his brother, trying to teach him a lesson, to take some responsibility. If only Alex—

The door opened, someone came in.

Adam sat up in the bed. It was Alex.

"Who is it?" Cassie mumbled, turning to look toward the door, holding the covers to her throat. "*Alex?* What are you doing here?"

Alex simply stood by the door and stared. He looked numb and shaken.

Adam could tell something was wrong. *Terribly* wrong. But he couldn't even get out of bed and go to his brother because he had nothing on and nothing to put on.

"What's the matter, Alex?" he asked, dreading the answer.

"I told her," he said simply. "And I came here to tell you that it was okay to tell Cassie. But I see you already have." He attempted a smile, but it turned out strange and twisted. "I wish Kelly had been as understanding as Cassie. The wedding's off, Adam. It was just like I feared. She called the wedding off."

"Sit down, Alex," Adam said, stretching out a hand as if he could physically detain him that way. He pulled on the sheet until it was free, leaving Cassie the comforter for cover, then wrapped it around his waist. "I think I've got some extra clothes in the back of the closet."

Alex obediently dropped into a nearby chair, hung his head and stared at his hands. He was obviously devastated.

While Adam looked for something to put on, he snatched glimpses of Cassie out the corner of his eye. He found it very strange that after her initial "What are you doing here?" she hadn't asked another question. Hadn't said another word. It was as though she already knew. Already understood. He remembered how she'd pulled away after their lovemaking and got a sick feeling in his stomach.

Could she know? Did she understand exactly what was going on? Why Alex was there? And if she did...would she understand why he and Alex had chosen to lie and forgive him for it? That was the question that would gnaw at him until he got a chance to talk with her.

Adam took the musty-smelling clothes he found and put them on in the bathroom. When he came out again, Alex was still sitting silently and Cassie was propped against some pillows, watching him with a sad expression. He hoped that meant she'd have similar feelings of sympathy for *him*...jerk that he was! He knew he'd done something horrible and didn't deserve forgiveness. But forgiveness was exactly what he hoped and prayed for.

"I'm going to take Alex back to his place so we can talk."

Cassie looked down and nodded.

"I may have to stay with him for a while."

"I understand."

"And when I get back, I'll explain all of this to you."

She nodded again.

"Cassie?"

She looked up slowly, reluctantly. He couldn't tell

what she was thinking, feeling. She seemed remote, fenced off. It scared the hell out of him!

"I was going to tell you before..."

Dully, she said, "I guess you tried."

"Yes."

She looked down again.

"I'd better get Alex home. I'll be back as soon as I can, but go ahead and get some sleep. It may be morning before you see me again."

He didn't expect her to reply and she didn't. He moved to the chair where Alex was slumped and pulled him to his feet. As they were leaving, Cassie surprised him by calling out Alex's name instead of his.

They both turned.

"I'm sorry about Kelly," she said simply.

Alex nodded, tried to smile, then turned and stepped into the rain. Adam followed.

It was a long night. Adam really hadn't expected Kelly to call off the wedding. He had expected anger and tears and maybe a postponement. But his faith had been so strong in the love Kelly and Alex had for each other, he believed they'd somehow work it out and the wedding would go on. He believed, and he still did, that truth between them—even when it was late in coming—was more important than ignorant bliss. But so far Kelly wasn't appreciating this distinction.

Adam understood her initial distrust and disillusionment. She would be wondering why Alex felt the need to lie in the first place. Was it really because he was afraid he'd lose her or alienate her parents? Or was it because he still had feelings for Cassie?

Adam tried to convince Alex that Kelly just needed time. Time to sort through her feelings, time to realize she loved him enough to forgive and trust him again. Alex needed to be patient.

But patience was a hard virtue to press on a man on the eve of his canceled wedding day. There was nothing to look forward to in the morning but humiliation and the disappointment of dozens of family members who had come to share the most important day of his life. They would blame him, and he deserved it.

Adam and Alex watched the sun come up at 4:35, sipping coffee in Alex's kitchen. They'd talked all night and had downed a pot of java between them just to keep them going for the difficult day ahead.

"Are you going to be okay?"

Alex smiled grimly. "Unfortunately, yes. It would be easier if I just gave up, quit eating and faded away to nothing. But I'm not going to give up on Kelly. Somehow I'll get through this nightmare and try again."

Adam smiled. "It's good to hear you talk this way. I hope it's not just the caffeine."

Alex chuckled. "Could be a little bit. Oh, I'll still have some tough times, Adam. But as long as you can talk me through the worst of it, I'll manage."

Adam stood up and thumped Alex on the shoulder with his open hand. "If I'm around, I'm yours."

Alex frowned and looked up at his brother. "Maybe I shouldn't have taken you away from Cassie last night...just when I did. You've still got to make things right with her."

Adam nodded. "Wish me luck. I'll need it."

"I do wish you luck, Adam. I should never have dragged you into this in the first place."

"I'm a big boy. You didn't twist my arm."

"But when you wanted to end it sooner, I wouldn't let you. I was a real bastard."

"Yes, you were. But you were scared. You weren't yourself."

"Lord, I *hope* that wasn't me!"

"Gotta go," Adam said, peering through the window at the lightening day. "Glad it's not raining."

"Yeah, Mom and Dad can display my head on a stake in bright sunshine."

"I'm sure they'll sharpen a stake for *my* head, too, Alex. See you later, dead or alive."

Alex pushed himself to his feet with a weary sigh and followed Adam to the door. Adam opened it, and they both stared at the person standing on the other side.

"Hi, Alex," Kelly said, pale and pink-eyed but with a tremulous smile. "Can I come in?"

ADAM DROVE home with renewed hope in his heart. Maybe there'd be a wedding after all! It was certainly a good sign that Kelly was there bright and early on Adam's doorstep and not carrying a gun!

It gave him hope for his own situation, too. He hadn't had a chance yet to explain himself to Cassie. He didn't even know how much she already knew, but he was certain she knew enough to be hurt and angry.

Cassie was really the one with the most to feel hurt about. The fact that the whole deceit had involved the most precious thing in her life—her son—would make it difficult for her to forgive. She was fiercely maternal. It was just one of the things that made her so lovable, so wonderful.

Adam's heart was in his throat as he pulled into his driveway. He wasn't sure if she'd be in the guest cabin or in the main house. It was still early, so he tried the cabin first.

He walked in, her name on his lips. But the bed was empty. And made.

Terror gripping him, he moved to the closet and threw it open. Just as he feared, Cassie's clothes were gone.

There was still a chance she was at the main house. After all, how could they have got out of there without assistance? The ferry didn't run between 1:00 a.m. and 5:00 a.m. and neither of them could fly. Of course, Kelly had somehow gotten over from Kenai. Where there was a will there was a way, he supposed. But it wasn't exactly an inspiring or comforting thought just at that moment.

He hurried into the house and...found his father sitting at the table. His heart sank to his toes.

"Dad."

"Adam."

"You flew them out?"

"As soon as the rain stopped around two-thirty."

Adam nodded, weariness and misery threatening to overcome him.

"Come and have some coffee, son. I expect I need to do for you what you just did for Alex."

Adam was grateful for his dad's support, but the one big difference between his hope for happiness and Alex's—a difference his father could never fix—was the absence of a woman at the door, asking…"Can I come in?"

As THE PLANE approached the Billings airport, Cassie looked out over the familiar countryside with an aching but grateful heart. This was *home*. It wasn't as lush and majestic as the Kenai Peninsula, but it had its own brand of wide-open beauty, rugged mountains and endless skies. Here she hoped she'd find peace of mind again, settle into the life she knew and loved before this dreamlike detour to Alaska.

She turned to observe her father, just waking from a nap, and Tyler between them, still sleeping. The last twenty-four hours had been exhausting for all of them, especially Ty. He'd been awakened in the middle of the night for the trip to Anchorage, then they'd had to wait in the airport for hours for the next flight to San Francisco and another to Montana. That's what happened when three people who weren't scheduled to fly out until the next day decided to go standby. Her father called it the hurry-up-and-wait dilemma.

Now it was nearly eight o'clock, the long purple shadows of the evening creeping over the landscape. The sun went down here at nine o'clock at the latest in early summer, unlike Alaska, the land of the midnight sun, where everything incredibly beautiful was illuminated until the night was nearly over.

Incredibly beautiful. Like Adam's face as he'd

looked down at her in the midst of their lovemaking. The curve of his throat from that angle, the loving expression in his eyes. How could she have ever mistaken one brother for the other? In Adam's lovemaking there had been such a depth of tenderness and meaning. He and Alex were *so* different...

Yet, in one respect, too much alike. They had conspired together to dupe her into believing a lie that made things simpler, easier for them.

She'd meant it when she told Alex she was sorry about Kelly. Sorry that he'd lost Kelly because of *her*. She truly believed he loved his fiancée—and dreaded the influence of his formidable in-laws—and perhaps that's why he'd resorted to such a deceitful trick. But that didn't excuse it.

Cassie just wished she'd never set eyes on that magazine, never written to Adam, never gone to Alaska. If she hadn't, the wedding would have gone on as planned. Alex would have lived his life ignorant of the fact that he was father to the most wonderful little boy in the world. But Cassie knew that *she* had received the greater blessing in knowing and loving Tyler, in having him a part of her life forever.

As for Adam...

Cassie wasn't sure why she couldn't feel the same compassion for Adam, the same understanding. She supposed he was only trying to help his brother. But because of what had happened between them—not just the physical lovemaking, but the bonding with Tyler, the friendship that had so quickly blossomed into love—his lies seemed like the worst kind of betrayal.

He'd said he wanted to talk to her last night, before they'd made love, and maybe he was going to tell her the truth then. She didn't know. She'd never know. Would it have made any difference?

As the airplane wheels hit the runway, Cassie looked at the tinted windows of the terminal. Somewhere in there Brad was waiting for them. Faithful, bighearted Brad.

Brad would never lie to her.

Chapter Twelve

The wedding was on. Kelly and Alex still had some talking to do, but they were committed to working everything out between them because a most important and vital fact remained: they loved each other deeply.

So, they kept their overnight rift to themselves, confiding the particulars of it to only two people besides those directly involved. Other than Kelly, Alex, Adam, Cassie and Jasper, only Peter and Monica were privy to the fact that Tyler was Alex's biological son, not Adam's. And that's the way they planned to keep it…if Adam agreed.

As Alex and Adam dressed for the wedding, they had time to talk this over.

"So, *why* do you still want everyone to think I'm Ty's father?" Adam demanded to know, astonished at such an idea, particularly after everything they'd been through.

All dressed in his tuxedo except for his jacket, Alex was adjusting his bow tie in front of the small, square mirror over the dresser in their old bedroom in the folks' house in Homer. Two twin beds still rested at opposite sides of the room, pennants hung on the walls along with posters and pictures from their teenage years. Adam, fully dressed, sat on the bed that used to be his, fiddling with a cuff link.

Alex turned with a serious expression on his face. "Don't worry, bro, I'm not trying to weasel out of anything here. I never intended to be a father to Tyler. You know I'm not the fatherly type. Kelly and I may *never* have children. She thinks they're cute, but that's as far as it goes. And the people who *should* know I'm Tyler's biological parent have already been told. Kelly knows the truth and so do the folks. As for Kelly's parents," he added wryly, "we've decided that they're on a need-to-know-only basis. Those two have the unenlightened mentality of the Dark Ages."

Adam couldn't disagree about the Armstrongs, but he still had reservations. "But I wonder what Cassie would think about this? Would she think it was still an act of deceit just to make things easier for you?"

Alex raised his brows. "I don't know. But if you're worried about it, why don't you call her and ask her what she thinks? She'd probably be thrilled to know that Kelly and I worked things out."

"Oh, that was smooth, Alex," Adam drawled. "I suppose you think that would be a clever way to insinuate myself back into Cassie's life. I don't think she'd even talk to me. In fact, I don't think I'll ever see her again."

"Well, if that's how you feel, why are you worried about what Cassie thinks, anyway?"

"It's the principle of the thing," Adam insisted.

"We've handled that end of it, bro," Alex argued. "Like I said, the people who matter, the people who have a right to know the truth, have been told. As far as Tyler's future goes, it's no longer important who supplied him with the Baranof genes. That's been established. In an impulsive and irresponsible act of romantic lust, *I* did."

"Don't remind me," Adam muttered.

"Does that mean he should be chained to a father like *me* forever? Hell, I should hope not. Biology doesn't make a man a real father. Love does. And if I ain't mistakin', bro, you grew real fond of that kid while he was here."

"Well, sure, I *care* about Tyler, but I'm not—"

"But you could be. As far as I'm concerned, Adam, Tyler's yours."

Adam gave an incredulous bark of laughter. "With or without his mother's consent, I suppose?"

"You want him, don't you?"

Caught off guard, Adam blurted, "Sure, I do. I wished he was mine right from the beginning."

He immediately looked chagrined, but Alex smiled, satisfied to have so cleverly extracted the confession. He slipped into his tux jacket.

"Then what's the trouble?"

"Oh, some father I'd be a thousand miles away and with no access to the kid!" he exclaimed, standing up to pace the floor. "Cassie wouldn't let me within a hundred miles of him."

"Then it sounds to me like this—if you want to see your son, you'd better make up with his mother."

Adam sat down on the bed again, resting his elbows on his thighs and letting his hands dangle between his knees in a defeated pose. "She made her feelings pretty clear when she left without even giving me a chance to tell my side of the story...not that that would have helped much."

"Maybe she left because she loves you too much."

"Oh, sure. That makes a load of sense."

Alex turned back to the mirror and gave his bow tie a final tweak. "Think about it, bro. But if you haven't done anything to remedy this sad state of affairs by the time Kelly and I are back from Hawaii, I might have to take matters into my own hands."

Adam rose and stood behind his brother, their reflections identical except for Alex's black eye and Adam's scowl.

"I'll handle this *my* way, little brother."

"Which means, I suppose, not at all," Alex said with a sniff.

"Alex..."

Alex smiled. "Let's not quarrel on my wedding day, bro. It's a miracle it's taking place at all. Be happy for me."

Adam's scowl faded away and was replaced with a reluctant grin. "I *am* happy for you, Alex. Now shouldn't we be going?" He patted his coat pockets and the scowl reappeared. "Damn, I think I've lost the rings!"

"Adam..."

Now the grin was back. "Fooled ya."

A WEEK AFTER Cassie was home, she was rocking in the porch swing on a hot Saturday afternoon, drinking lemonade and waiting for Brad. It was the first day she'd taken off since returning to Nye and she was feeling extremely lazy. No, make that lethargic. No…make that *depressed*. No point in lying to herself.

She heard the screen door open behind her and looked up at her father. "Ty asleep?"

"Yep."

"Good." She took another sip and pushed off with one dangling foot for another languorous swing.

"He wanted to stay up and see his Uncle Brad, but I told 'im you and Brad had some private talkin' to do."

Cassie smiled faintly, her half-closed eyes watching the dusty road beyond the fence. "How did that go over?"

"Not too bad, actually. He figures you and Brad are fixin' to set the weddin' date."

Cassie was startled out of her listlessness. She gazed up at her father. "Where did he get that idea?"

"Don't know. But I reckon we need to sit him down one day soon and give him the lowdown with no frills attached."

Cassie turned to watch the road again. "You mean tell him that I'm not going to marry Brad…ever?"

Cassie waited nervously through the long pause that followed. Finally her father muttered gruffly, "Cassandra Montgomery, don't tell me you've changed your mind about Brad…*again!*"

Cassie hitched up one shoulder and ever so

slightly shoved out her bottom lip. "Well, I don't know. It's just that I've been thinking lately—"

"Cassandra, look at me."

When her father used that tone of voice, Cassie obeyed. Jasper looked as grim as an undertaker. "Er…yeah, Dad?"

"If you're thinkin' what I think you're thinkin', you got another think coming."

"What's *that* supposed to mean?"

"You don't love Brad. You told me so yourself. And I know for certain that you're in love with someone else."

Cassie turned away, blinking back tears that came on suddenly at the slightest, most distant allusion to *that man in Alaska*. The nights were the worst, though. The quiet darkness offered no interruptions for her traitorous thoughts of missed kisses and looks and wonderful times spent together. "I've learned that love is highly overrated. I much prefer a man I can depend on, a man who will tell me the truth, *always*."

"Hell, Cassie, no one tells the truth all the time."

"But the size of the lies makes a big difference."

"Even good men make mistakes."

Cassie turned her head sharply to glare at her father. "I suppose you're going to tell me that you think Adam Baranof is a good man?"

Jasper nodded. "Damn right I am. You asked me to give him a chance and I did. I found out real fast that I liked the boy."

"He's no boy and…and he knew better."

"I think that's what he was planning to tell you last Saturday night when you were hell-bent on hightailing it out of there faster than a jackrabbit in heat.''

"Tell me what? That he knew better?''

Jasper nodded again. "Yep. That boy suffered over it. Tellin' lies didn't sit well with 'im. I could see that, easy.''

"Then he shouldn't have agreed to cover for his brother in the first place.''

"Yep. I'm sure he knew that about three minutes after the fact.''

Cassie gave an exasperated hiss. "Dad, why are you sticking up for him? It's *over!*''

Jasper snorted. "Is it?'' Then before Cassie could launch another flurry of arguments, he continued, "But, as far as Brad's concerned, it doesn't really matter what's goin' on with you and Adam. You don't love Brad and it'd be damned selfish of you to keep danglin' that carrot in front of his nose, Cassie. Cut 'im loose, hon. Cut 'im loose. It's the humane thing to do.''

After regaling her with his horse analogies, Jasper left Cassie to stew. But it didn't take her long to admit that, no matter how it had been put into words, her father was right. When Brad came, she'd have to cut 'im loose.

She wasn't sure why she had even been considering dangling that carrot a second longer. She knew she wasn't in love with Brad and never would be, and simply feeling secure with him because he was trustworthy and devoted wasn't enough of a reason—for *either* of them—to hang on to a going-nowhere relationship.

In the past week Cassie had avoided talking to

Brad by working late at the store almost every day, then coming home to spend a couple of hours with Tyler before going to bed exhausted. The exhaustion hadn't helped her sleep or block out the constant thoughts of Adam, but the nonstop busyness had at least helped her cope during the daylight hours. Susan watched her slave away at the store and clicked her tongue, but no amount of sympathy or advice from her faithful friend slowed Cassie down.

She just couldn't sort out all the confusing thoughts and feelings! How could she be so in love and so hurt at the same time? How could she want him every minute, yet wish he didn't exist?

Five minutes later, Brad's truck passed through the front gate and pulled to a stop in front of the house. Cassie watched him swing his long legs out of the cab and saunter up the sidewalk to the porch. She shook her head with rueful wonder. He had a damned sexy saunter, but it didn't get to her in the least. What was the matter with her! Most women would give their eyeteeth for a suitor with a sexy saunter like Brad's!

Lean and tan and leggy in snug jeans, his fresh-washed blond hair glinting in the sun, he was a fine figure of a man. Why she was able to appreciate this fact and still be completely unmoved was a mystery to Cassie. Brad needed and deserved a woman who couldn't wait to peel off those jeans and get down to business.

"Hi." He smiled and sat down in the swing beside her, smelling faintly of aftershave. Brad was subtle, right down to the nice way he smelled.

"Hi." She smiled back. "Want some lemonade?"

"No thanks. Just had a soda."

She set her own half-empty glass of lemonade on a nearby patio table and waited for him to get the ball rolling. For once, she didn't feel very comfortable with Brad, and she sensed that he was feeling the same way.

"Cassie—"

"Brad—"

They laughed. "You go first," she offered.

"Maybe you should go first since you're the one who invited me over to talk. I can't believe we haven't managed to get together since I drove you home from the airport."

"I've kept busy at work…on purpose, I guess. But I figured you deserved an explanation about why we went to Alaska. I knew you didn't buy that sudden urge to go on a vacation bit."

"No, but I figured you'd tell me in time. I figured it had something to do with Tyler's father, and I knew that was something you've fretted about over the years."

Cassie smiled wryly. "Yes, but I'd have been better off if I'd just kept on frettin'."

Brad got an understanding look in his eyes. "I know."

"You do? Did Dad—?"

"No, it wasn't your father that told me the whole story…."

"Then who? The only other soul I confided in was—"

"Susan," he finished for her, looking chagrined.

"Susan?" Cassie repeated blankly.

"Yeah, Susan. She said you didn't swear her to secrecy, so she figured it was okay to fill me in. Especially since you were going to tell me sooner or later, anyway."

Cassie shook her head in confusion. "But I didn't realize you even knew Susan. I mean, to talk to her and all."

Brad fidgeted a little, looked off toward the road as she'd done earlier while talking with her father. "We both like to eat lunch over at B.J.'s now and then. It seemed silly to sit at different tables." Gazing at Brad's profile, Cassie could swear she detected a blush on those high cheekbones. "At first we just talked about *you.* Then, after a while..."

Suddenly Cassie was getting the picture. Instead of cuttin' Brad loose, Brad was cuttin' *her* loose! "Brad, are you and Susan—?"

His self-conscious look told all.

She couldn't help an astonished laugh. "You *are* talking about my Susan, the Susan who works for me? The perky brunette?"

"The same."

"Well, why didn't you tell me? Why didn't you *say* something?"

He stared at her as if he weren't sure whether she was happy or mad. At first Cassie wasn't sure, either. It was such a shock!

"In the beginning there was nothing to tell you. Just an innocent little lunch now and then with a nice girl. And, as I said, we talked about you mostly. I think she felt sorry for me 'cause you couldn't make up your mind about us."

Cassie suddenly remembered about Susan's eager defense of Brad on the day they'd found Adam's picture in the magazine, not to mention her eagerness to get Cassie to consider a hot hunk from Alaska in the first place!

"It was a gradual thing, Cassie. I was pretty confused for a while. I've always cared for you, you know that. But I've come to care for Susan, too, and it's…it's *different*. It made me realize that you and I just weren't meant to be." He reached over and took her hand. "But I think you've known that for a while. And this trip to Alaska just made it more obvious to you, didn't it?"

Cassie smiled. She couldn't believe that she was getting off the hook so easily, and, in the process, two people she cared a whole lot about were going to be supremely happy. Well, she was certainly glad her father had made her see sense before she'd made a fool of herself with Brad by sending marriage signals to a man already taken. Sometimes things actually *did* work out.

Cassie squeezed Brad's hand. "I'm happy for you, Brad. And Susan, too. Are we going to be hearing wedding bells any time soon?"

He got a dreamy look in his eyes that made Cassie just a little bit jealous. Not of Susan, but of the happiness she and Brad had found with each other.

"Not *real* soon. Maybe…I don't know… Christmas."

"You make a great couple and I'm sure you'll be very happy."

"Thanks, Cass." His brow furrowed. "But what about Tyler? What will he think about all this?"

Cassie chewed her bottom lip. Brad had asked a very good question. Was Tyler going to miss more than Jolly Ranchers if Brad wasn't in his life?

FOR ONCE in his life, Jasper was taken completely by surprise. "You're kiddin' me."

"No, I'm not."

"I don't believe it."

"Believe it."

"Brad and *Susan?* Hell, I thought he was in love with *you.*"

"He thought he was, too, till recently. Susan changed his mind about that."

Cassie and Jasper were in the dining room. Dinner was over and Ty and Sylvie were in the kitchen getting ice cream and cookies for dessert.

"Why didn't he say something to *me?*" Jasper wondered.

"Come on, Dad, you're the last person he'd tell that he was falling out of love with your daughter. No...he was never *really* in love with me in the first place. Too bad Tyler somehow got the idea that Brad and I were destined to marry."

"Cass, I never actually *said*—"

"I know you didn't, Dad. But Tyler's smart. He picked up vibes from all of us, and he probably heard other people talking, too."

"Well, just because Brad's gonna be married doesn't mean they can't still be buds."

"Over time things will change. It's inevitable, Dad. But Tyler's growing up anyway and he'll be going to school soon. Besides, he'll always have you."

Jasper smiled and patted Cassie's hand resting on the table. He didn't say anything, but Cassie knew what he was thinking. No, Tyler wouldn't *always* have him and it was too bad Ty didn't have a father. But he'd never dream of expecting Cassie to marry simply to supply Tyler with a father. And she had *finally* come to realize that she would never dream of settling for anything less than what she and Ty both deserved—a man they both loved, a man that loved them both.

Funny how Adam suddenly came to mind...

Tyler and Sylvie returned with chocolate ice cream scooped into bowls and homemade oatmeal cookies. After settling Ty in his chair and handing around the bowls, Sylvie headed back to the kitchen.

"Stay and have some ice cream, Sylvie," Jasper called. "There's only a few hundred grams of fat and a cup of sugar in each bowl." Sylvie was as slim as a reed and had the energy of an army, but she refused to eat dessert because she was sure it would make her fat. Jasper loved to tease her about it...among many other things.

"It'd all go to my hips," Sylvie informed them, bustling away. "Besides, I've got dishes to do!"

"I'm glad I don't care about fat 'n sugar," Tyler said complacently as he ate another spoonful of ice cream.

"Me, too, bud," Jasper said.

Cassie watched Tyler eating his favorite dessert and wondered if this might be a good time to break the news about Brad. She telegraphed her intentions to Jasper and he nodded his head in agreement.

"Did Granddad tell you I was going to have a talk with Uncle Brad today?"

Tyler peered at her over his bowl, his nose tipped with chocolate ice cream. He scooped in another bite and mumbled, "Uh-huh."

"Granddad said you were sort of expecting Uncle Brad to ask me to marry him."

Ty's eyes got big. "Did he?"

Cassie shook her head. "No, Ty, he didn't. In fact, I think he's going to marry my friend, Susan. You know the nice lady who works with me at the bookstore?"

"Really?" He seemed momentarily arrested, but not disappointed or unhappy. Then he asked, "Can I have some more ice cream?"

Cassie exchanged a surprised look with Jasper. "So, you don't mind if Uncle Brad marries Susan? You weren't hoping he'd be…you know…a part of *our* family?" She purposely left out the word *daddy*.

Tyler screwed up his face, considering. Finally he said, "I like Uncle Brad a lot and I wouldn't mind if he was my daddy. But I figure there's other uncles you can choose from, Mommy, someone *you* might like better, like Uncle Adam. *I* really like him, too. But don't marry Uncle Alex, 'cause he wouldn't make a good daddy at all."

For a moment, Cassie was speechless. How could such a small boy be so perceptive, so wise? He'd easily picked up on the fact that Alex wasn't daddy material, and that Adam was. And that *she* liked Uncle Adam, too…against her better judgment.

Tyler didn't know the whole story. He didn't know there were chinks in Adam's armor. He didn't know that to pass muster Adam had to be as good at being a husband as he was at being a daddy.

Cassie fought the dull and dreadful ache that crept into her heart every time she faced the possibility of her and Tyler's dream never coming true. Adam might easily fit the bill as a daddy, but the husband part was extremely doubtful. Even if she could bring herself to forgive him, to trust him again, he might not have the slightest intention of committing himself to such a permanent arrangement as marriage.

So her whole Hamletesque agony over "to forgive or not to forgive" might be a moot point. Maybe Adam didn't care either way. After all, it had been a week since she left Alaska and he hadn't bothered to call or write or—

"Well, Mommy?"

Cassie blinked. "What, honey?"

"*Can* I have some more ice cream?"

Feeling foolish for drifting into her own tortured little world, she smiled and said, "Sure, hon. But just half a bowl. Go on into the kitchen and tell Sylvie I said it was okay."

"Thanks, Mom!" He was gone in a flash.

"No childhood angst troublin' that kid," Jasper said proudly. "Don't worry about 'im, Cass. He'll take whatever's dished 'im."

"Especially if it's chocolate flavored," Cassie said wryly.

LATER, AFTER Sylvie went home, Cassie, Jasper and Tyler put an old forties cowboy movie in the VCR and settled in the cozy family room at the back of the house to watch it. When the phone rang during an especially loud barroom shoot-out, Cassie said to Jasper, "That might be Susan. If it is, I'll probably be a while." Then she went into the kitchen to answer it.

"Hello?"

"Hello, Cassie. Don't hang up…*please.*"

Chapter Thirteen

"Kelly, is that you?"

"Yeah, it's me. Please don't hang up!"

"Why would I hang up on *you?*" Cassie gave a nervous little chuckle. "You didn't lie to me."

"No, but you might think I'm a traitor. I forgave Alex for lying to me and we went ahead and got married on Sunday."

"You *did?* Oh, Kelly, I'm so happy for you!" And she really meant it. "I felt so bad about showing up at the worst possible time and causing so much trouble for you."

"Well, that wasn't your fault. If Alex had told me the truth—told us *both* the truth—right at the beginning, things would have been so much easier. We could have dealt with it together. It was his lying that made things so complicated."

"And Adam's lying," Cassie added quietly.

"Well, I think that Adam, at least, has learned his lesson," Kelly said in an aggravated tone. "But Alex is on his way to your house right now with another scheme up his sleeve."

Cassie's eyes widened. "What do you mean, another scheme? And why aren't you two on your honeymoon?''

"Alex cut the honeymoon short, if you can believe it.''

"But why?''

"He's been too worried about Adam.''

Cassie's heart seemed to leap into her throat. "What's...what's wrong with Adam? He isn't hurt or sick or—''

"Just lovesick over you.''

Faintly Cassie said, "Oh.''

"Before we left for Hawaii, Alex tried to talk Adam into calling you to try to work things out, but Adam didn't think you'd give him the time of day. But Alex can't be happy if Adam isn't, and since he blames himself for dragging Adam into this in the first place, Alex decided this morning to fly down there to Montana and do Adam's talking for him. And I mean that literally.''

"Literally?''

"I mean, he's going to pose as Adam.''

Cassie was stunned. "He actually told you he was going to do that?''

"He doesn't lie to me anymore, Cassie. He told me exactly what he planned to do. And he promised me that it would be the last time he'd ever do anything like this again. He justified it because he wants to help Adam. Sound familiar, only the other way around?''

Cassie gave a helpless chuckle. "Those two get in more trouble that way. Why didn't you tell Adam so he could stop Alex?''

"I called his house all morning, no answer. Then

I went over there and saw the plane was gone, so I figure he went to Anchorage or something. When I couldn't get hold of Adam, I decided at the last minute to call you."

"What do you mean the last minute?"

"Alex could show up there any second. I just thought you should be prepared."

"Well, thanks for calling, Kelly, but I don't have a clue what to do."

There was a pause, then, "Can I give you some advice?"

"Er...okay."

"Give Alex a lecture for trying to scam you and send him home with his tail between his legs. The only way we're ever going to tame the brothers Baranof is by putting them in their place whenever they try something crazy like this. *Then...*"

Cassie laughed. "Then?"

"Then send Alex home with a message for Adam. Tell him you forgive him. Believe me, Cass—" Her voice got soft and dreamy "—forgiveness has its rewards."

Cassie sobered. "I don't know, Kelly. I'd *like* to forgive him, but—"

"You care about him, don't you?"

"Yes, but—"

The doorbell rang and Cassie nearly jumped out of her skin. "Oh m'gosh, he's here," she whispered into the phone.

"Call me later, Cass," Kelly said. "And good luck."

Cassie nodded into the phone as if Kelly could see her, then hung up. Suddenly her palms were sweaty and her heart was beating out of her chest. It was only Alex at the door, but he *looked* like Adam, and that, apparently, was enough to get her all worked up. And the very idea that he thought he could pose as Adam and actually fool her into believing him...! She was going to do exactly what Kelly advised and send him home feeling as low as a scolded puppy.

She hurried through the dark living room, not bothering to turn on lights. She opened the door and, barely looking at him, grabbed Alex's arm before he could say a word and dragged him across the porch and around to the side of the house. Under the thick branches of a huge old elm tree that blocked most of the moonlight from getting through, Cassie faced her foe.

"Alex Baranof, how *dare* you?"

The dark outline of a man shaped alarmingly like Adam spread his arms wide. "Cassie, it's me. It's Adam!"

She shook her finger in his face. "Don't try to pull that stunt on me, Alex. I know what you're up to and you should be ashamed!"

"Cassie—"

Cassie glanced nervously at the house, at the lighted window of the family room. "Keep your voice down, Alex. I don't want Dad or Tyler to even know you're here. When will you ever learn your lesson? You should never have gotten Adam to take your place as Tyler's father, and you taking his place now isn't right, either! I know you think you're only trying to help, but Adam should be here speaking for himself!"

Alex grabbed her shoulders. "But, Cassie, I *am*—"

Cassie wriggled out of Alex's grasp and turned her back on him, crossing her arms over her chest. "Not that speaking for himself would do him any good, either. I mean, how could he have lied about something as important as Tyler's paternity?"

"That was terrible and I'm sorry."

"It's not enough that *you're* sorry, Alex. Adam needs to be sorry. Sure, Kelly says he's sorry. You say he's sorry. But I need to hear it from *him*."

Cassie kept her back to Alex, stewing, while he remained silent. There was a soft breeze in the air, gently rustling the leaves in the branches overhead. Finally Alex spoke again in a low, measured tone. "So, are you saying that if…if Adam had actually come down here to see you, to say he was sorry, to promise never to lie to you again even about something as silly and inconsequential as a parking ticket, you might…forgive him?"

Cassie kicked at a tuft of grass. "I *might*. But he didn't."

"What if he did?"

Cassie shrugged. "I don't know. He really hurt me."

Alex gave a long, shaky sigh. "I'm sorry about that."

"But is *he* sorry?"

When he spoke again, he was standing so close to her Cassie actually felt his breath on her neck. An unexpected chill went down her back. "Cassie, I *am* Adam."

She whirled on him, furious. "Alex, quit pretending!"

His head fell back and his hands came up in a frustrated pose. "Why do you persist in thinking I'm Alex?"

"Kelly called me. I *know,* Alex. You don't have to keep putting on a show. Besides, you're wasting your time. If Adam really cared you wouldn't be here in the first place."

There was a pause, then he said, "Wait, let's go back to that first part. You said Kelly called you?"

"Yes, but don't be mad at her, Alex. She was just trying to keep you from messing things up again."

"Kelly said that Alex was coming *here?*"

Cassie couldn't help it. She was reluctantly impressed. "You know, you really *are* good at this. Maybe you should have gone into acting instead of marine geology. But save your theatrics for community theater, Alex, because this audience isn't buying your act."

Again Alex fell silent. Cassie couldn't quite see his face in the dark, just the occasional glint of moonlight reflected in his eyes, but she could feel the intensity of his emotions. She decided he must really be guilt-stricken over the situation. But you couldn't fix a bad situation created by lying by telling more lies!

"Can I ask you something, Cass?"

Alex's tone of voice gave Cassie a flutter in her stomach. He sounded almost tender. He sounded *so* much like Adam.

"What?" She knew she was being sulky, but she

couldn't help it. Having Alex there just made her miss Adam all the more.

"What makes you so sure Adam doesn't care about you?"

"Well, to begin with—"

"I know what you're going to say...*he isn't here.* But think back to the time you spent with him in Alaska."

That's all Cassie had been thinking about for the past week! She shook her head firmly. "There's no point in—"

"Do you remember the way he looked at you?"

"What do you mean?"

"The way he couldn't take his eyes off you? The expression in his eyes?"

Cassie thought about Adam's eyes and the way he used to look at her. She was lost in delicious thought until Alex brought her back to reality, then sent her floating on a cloud again with his next question. "What about the way he kissed you? You could tell how he felt about you then, couldn't you? It was different with him, different than it was with...with me, different than it was with any other man."

"All two of them," Cassie admitted with a sigh, then added wistfully, "Different than it would have been with any guy, I suppose."

"Then maybe this will convince you."

Before Cassie knew what was happening, Alex grabbed her shoulders and pulled her against his chest.

"Alex, what are you doing?"

"For the last time," he growled as he wrapped

his arms around her so tightly she could barely breathe, much less struggle out of his embrace, "I am *not* Alex, and I am going to kiss you!"

"This is crazy! This isn't right! This is—"

Despite turning her head from side to side and trying to kick him in the shins with flailing feet, Alex's lips captured hers. It took about two seconds to realize that, once again, she'd confused one Baranof brother with the other.

This is Adam, her heart told her.

She quit fighting and started participating. The kiss combined the excitement of coming home and the thrill of taking off on a wonderful adventure at the same time. The familiar feel of Adam's lips, Adam's arms around her, Adam's thick, silky hair to weave her eager fingers through, was heaven.

They parted at last, both spent of breath, both still clinging to each other like survivors of a catastrophe. But, in a way, that's what they were.

"Now, before either of us say another word, before we kiss again…tell me, Cassie, *who am I?*"

Cassie was tempted to tease, but she could tell how important this was to him. "You're Adam Baranof," she said softly, one finger tracing the slightly stubbly line of his jaw. "The man with the smooth chest. The man who preceded his troublesome twin brother into the world by three minutes."

He pulled her into a fierce, joyful hug. "Oh, Cassie, I've missed you so much! But I was afraid to call. Afraid you wouldn't talk to me."

"I've been so confused and hurt, I might not have," she admitted.

He grasped her shoulders and peered into her

face, struggling to see in the dark. "But you'll talk to me now?"

She dropped her forehead against his chest and chuckled deep in her throat. "Well I suppose we can't just kiss twenty-four hours a day."

He cupped her chin with his hand and gently urged her to look at him. In the dark she couldn't see, but she knew his eyes glowed with love. It radiated from him. "We could try," he teased.

She laughed, then he said, soberly, sincerely, "I *am* sorry, Cassie. We do need to talk. I'll tell you everything. I won't leave a detail out. I never want anything between us again but the truth."

She snuggled closer. "I never want anything between us again, period," she murmured.

They kissed again, and time stood still...until they heard a car approaching the house.

"I'll bet that's Alex," Cassie whispered. "What should we do? Read him the riot act for pretending to be you?"

"No, he hasn't done that yet. Maybe we should just wait and see what he does. Hurry, Cass! You go and meet him before he rings the doorbell. Don't let him know I'm here. Just play along for a while."

Cassie didn't have time to think about whether or not what Adam was proposing was a good idea. She heard the car door slam and knew Alex—if it really was him—was already headed to the house. She hurried around to the front—yeah, it was Alex, all right—just as he was climbing the three steps to the porch. Standing clear of the tree, the moonlight shined on her fully.

"Cassie?" Alex said, a little startled. "Is that you?"

"Yes, it's me. What are you doing here?" Cassie decided she wouldn't address him as Alex or Adam. She'd let him dig his own grave.

Cassie had stopped about fifteen feet away from Alex, crossed her arms over her chest and frowned. He started toward her, then stopped, as if discouraged by her unwelcoming pose. She could see him clearly in the porch light. All trace of the black eye was gone now, or hidden by makeup.

"Were you taking a walk?" he asked her in a meek and cajoling voice. He was stalling, of course. Maybe he was having second thoughts. Or maybe he was just easing into his "Adam act" slowly.

"Yes, I was walking. It's a beautiful night."

He nodded, licked his lips. "I guess you're pretty surprised to see me."

Interesting. He seemed just as reluctant to give himself a name as she was. She decided that maybe he was waiting for her to identify him one way or the other, taking his cue from her.

She wasn't about to make it easy for him, so she said, "Of course I'm surprised to see you, *Adam.* You haven't called or written since I saw you last weekend."

Your move, she thought.

By Alex's troubled expression, Cassie could tell he was having a mental struggle. Maybe his conscience was finally making itself painfully known. *About time.*

He released a long sigh. The struggle was over. "Cass, it's not Adam. It's me, Alex."

"Alex?"

"Don't sic your dad on me yet, Cass. Just listen to me."

"Why should I listen to you? You've done nothing but lie to me."

"Not anymore. I was going to tell you one more lie tonight, *one more* lie just to fix the mess I've made, but I couldn't do it. God, I'm so sorry! About everything!"

Cassie controlled her urge to smile. He sounded so contrite, so sincere! And it made her so happy! It was particularly gratifying to hear Alex's apology since Adam was hearing it, too, from his hiding place around the corner of the house.

When Cassie didn't answer, Alex continued in a more desperate tone. "If you can't forgive me, Cass, at least forgive Adam. That's really why I'm here. I came to plead my brother's case. I was actually going to pretend to be him, try to say all the right words to win you back."

"But why would you do that, Alex?"

"Because *I* was the one who dragged him into this mess in the first place! He's been digging *my* rear out of jams since we were kids, but this time I asked too much and he's paying for it. Cass, he's miserable without you. I've never seen him so much in I—"

"That's enough, Alex. I think I can speak for myself now."

Alex's eyes grew wide as Adam stepped out of the shadows to stand beside Cassie and wrap his arm around her shoulder.

"Adam! What are *you* doing here?"

"Little brother, I can ask you the same thing."

That silenced Alex for a minute, but only a minute. "You must have heard me just now! I haven't got ulterior motives, bro! I'm here to save your butt, just like you've saved mine a million times."

"I told you I could take care of my own business, didn't I, Alex?" Adam reminded him. "I told you not to interfere."

This was irrefutable, so Alex stuttered for a minute before blurting out, "You sure looked like you needed my help. You and your problems were all I could think about while Kelly and I were in Hawaii."

Adam grinned. "Well, then maybe you've been punished enough. The last thing a man wants to think about on his honeymoon is his brother. I sure as hell won't be thinking about *you* while I'm on *my* honeymoon!"

This announcement sent Cassie's circulatory system into overdrive. Her heart was racing, her head was pounding as blood surged through her body at the speed of light. Was Adam speaking hypothetically, or was this honeymoon something he planned for the near future with—dare she hope?—the likes of her?

Alex was wondering the same thing, but he had no trouble putting it succinctly into words. "Bro, are you and Cassie getting married?"

Adam's arm tightened around Cassie's shoulder, and it was a good thing because her knees got weak suddenly when he answered, "If she'll have me. But since I haven't yet asked, do you think you could give us a little time alone, Alex?"

Alex grinned from ear to ear. "I'd do a hip-hip-hooray, but I might attract coyotes. Or something even fiercer...like Cassie's dad."

"I've already been...er...attracted," came Jasper's voice from the front door. Cassie had forgotten that she'd flown out of the house so fast she'd left the front door open and only the screen door swinging closed behind her. How much had her father heard? And where was Tyler?

Alex looked horrified, but Jasper only laughed. "You look about as comfortable as a mongrel dog caught in the henhouse with feathers 'tween his teeth, Alex." He pushed open the screen door. "Come on in, son. You heard your brother. He wants a little private time with Cassie and, by damn, he's gonna get it. Ty's in the kitchen pourin' root beer and waitin' on me to pop some corn. We've got the second half of a shoot'em-up to watch. Care to join us?"

Alex knew this was not just an invitation, but a command. Still a little leery, but obviously without a choice in the matter, Alex gave a polite, nervous smile and preceded Jasper into the house.

"Straight down the hall to your right's the kitchen," he instructed Alex. "I'll be along in just a minute." Then he turned to Cassie and Adam.

"Since this might come up, Cassie," he began matter-of-factly, "I want you to know that I've got no problem with you and Ty moving to Alaska as long as I can spend part of each year there—the summer months, of course. The boy'll miss me and I'll miss him. Christmas you can come here. When we visit up there, you can give me and Sylvie the guest cabin.''

"You and *Sylvie?*" Cassie was stunned. How long had this been going on?

"Now that you're gonna be settled, Sylvie and I'll get married, too. I'll sell half the ranch to Brad and hire Jed Barlow as full-time manager to handle the other half. Me and my bride plan to travel quite a bit, y'see. So, now that you know how things'll be settled in *my* life, you go ahead and settle *your* life just exactly the way you want it...hear?''

"I—I hear, Dad," Cassie said in a quavery voice. She couldn't believe what was going on! It seemed as though everyone's lives around her had been in limbo until her own life had shifted into high gear and now they were *all* on paths to happiness! Brad and Susan, now her father and *Sylvie?* Boy, where had she been while all this was going on?

Jasper nodded with satisfaction. "Good. Now, take your time, you two. I'll keep the young'uns busy.''

Cassie and Adam laughed at the way Jasper lumped Alex and Ty into the same category. Fortunately Alex was too far away to hear. After Jasper went in, closing both doors behind him, Cassie turned to Alex. "I'm in shock," she said incredulously. "For so many reasons."

"You didn't know about Sylvie and your dad, I gather?''

"Not a clue."

"Well, your dad's a cagey guy. If he didn't want you to know, you wouldn't know.''

"But have *I* been the reason he hasn't married her already?"

"I don't know." Adam gave a crooked smile. "But I doubt either of them have been suffering...if you know what I mean. Marriage is probably just a formality for the wonderful, fulfilling relationship they already enjoy."

Cassie blushed and grinned ruefully. "Is that your way of hinting that they're sleeping together?"

"Like I said, your dad's a cagey guy. But let's not talk about Sylvie and Jasper, anymore. Let's talk about Cassie and Adam." Cassie was more than willing.

Adam took her hand and led her to the porch steps. He helped her to a seat on the top step, then lowered himself to the next step down. In the porch light, Cassie could see his handsome face clearly, see every expression, every tender gleam in his eye or smile on his kissable lips. If she hadn't dragged him into the shadows earlier, she'd have recognized him as Adam immediately.

But now he could see *her* just as clearly. Could he tell how nervous she was, how full of wonder and hope and surprise? Could he tell that she was about to burst with happiness, burst into tears, or both?

His smile was gentle, his eyes full of love and tender curiosity. "What are you thinking, Cassie? Have I bowled you over? Have I gone too fast? Talk to me, Cass. Tell me how you feel."

"I feel scared and nervous and happy and confused and never more sure of one thing..."

"And that is?"

"That I love you, Adam Baranof."

His smile stretched from ear to ear. His eyes glowed. "And I love you. In fact, I'm crazy about you. Does this mean…?"

He left the question dangling, but Cassie wouldn't settle for anything but a full proposal. With a teasing sternness, she said, "Adam Baranof, you sent your brother into the house with my father so we could be alone, so you could ask me a question. I've heard plenty of questions, but none of them particularly struck me as needing this kind of privacy. Maybe you'd better get to the point before Jasper and Ty hit the hay. You'll have to ask them *both* for my hand in marriage, you know."

Adam laughed. "I think your father already gave it."

"Adam!"

"But I'll get to the point, anyway." He got very serious, his mouth curved in the sweetest, sexiest smile. "It would give me the greatest pleasure— It would make me the happiest of men— Ah, hell, Cassie, *will* you marry me?"

Cassie's heart filled with joy. Sure it happened fast. But when it was meant to be, did that really matter?

Blinking back her tears, she answered, "Yes, Adam. I'll marry you."

They kissed to seal the deal, but Tyler's voice startled them apart. "Mommy?"

Cassie and Adam looked up to see Tyler standing at the threshold, one hand propping open the screen door, a very serious expression on his face. Jasper and Alex hovered in the background. Suddenly Cassie was nervous. What if, even after what he'd said earlier that night, Tyler didn't approve of her marriage to Adam? She could never do anything that made Tyler unhappy.

"What is it, honey?" she asked.

"Granddad said I wasn't supposed to bug ya, but I couldn't wait to ask Uncle Adam somethin'."

"What did you want to ask me, bud?" Adam said. By the way he was squeezing her hand, Cassie could tell he was nervous, too.

"I was just wonderin'…if you and my mommy get married, will you be my daddy for real or still jus' an uncle?"

"What do *you* want me to be, Ty?" he asked carefully.

Tyler shrugged. "Well, I want you to be my daddy, o' course."

Adam looked at Alex. Alex nodded and smiled. Adam looked at Cassie. She smiled, too, with tears in her eyes. "In that case, Ty, I'd be happy to be your daddy."

Ty's serious expression disappeared. He was beaming. "Good! When can we go fishin'?"

Epilogue

A year later

It was a crystal-blue June morning in Seldovia, a perfect day for fishing. Cassie wiped her wet hands on a dishcloth and looked out the back door toward the boat dock. Adam promised to have everyone back by eleven, time to clean the fish and cook it for lunch.

It was going to be a very special lunch for Cassie, not just because Dad and Sylvie had arrived from Montana the evening before, but because she had an announcement to make.

Cassie propped the heels of her hands against her lower back and stretched like a cat, pushing her bulging stomach out until it looked like a basketball. Cassie was only six months pregnant, but she felt as if she was ready to deliver any minute!

Incredibly, despite her extremely round middle, Adam still found her sexy. He didn't just say so, he showed her frequently. Cassie treasured their long, tender nights of lovemaking. But even when they just held each other and planned their family's rosy future, it was heaven just being in his arms. Cassie still felt like a honeymooner. She had never been so content.

As for Ty, after initially missing his Granddad to the point of a few teary episodes, he took to living in Alaska like a fish to water…the clichéd analogy entirely appropriate. Christmas in Montana did a great deal to speed the adjustment. It had been a wonderful holiday and a sort of confirmation to Tyler that his old home would always be there, complete with Granddad, his horse, Buster, and an especially glowing Sylvie these days…. It seemed marriage also worked a charm for the older generation. Cassie was grateful that Sylvie was filling a void for Jasper that her mother had left behind.

While in Nye for the holidays, they'd attended the wedding of one of Ty's "uncles," Uncle Brad and Susan. Susan now managed Cassie's bookstore and conferred with her via long-distance and E-mail on a daily basis. As long as Susan wanted to manage the store, Cassie would hold on to it. If Susan decided she wanted to buy the store or move on to something else, Cassie would sell.

By retaining ownership of the store, she had a ready excuse to talk to Susan frequently. It was so much fun to share anecdotes of marital bliss—and even to occasionally compare notes and give advice about the very rare not-so-blissful moments—with another newlywed. They were both happier than they ever thought possible.

Brad missed Ty, but he and Susan were working very hard at making a baby so Brad wouldn't be without a "bud" for too awfully long.

Christmas in Montana held special memories for Cassie in another respect, too. That's where she conceived her pregnancy, right there in her old bedroom where she used to have girlish dreams about the kind of man she was now actually married to, a man whom she enjoyed waking up with every morning and lying down to sleep with every night.

Well, except when he went out on two-to-three-week-long research treks, or was a guest speaker for some professor at Fairbanks University. Those occasions were difficult for Cassie, especially when the nights grew endlessly long in the winter. But she kept busy with Tyler, doing all kinds of indoor sports at the local gymnasium, as well as teaching him to read. There was no preschool in the area and he'd be attending kindergarten in the fall, so Cassie was making sure he was as prepared as every other child. Tyler was smart, so that was certainly no problem. He was just like his daddy in that respect.

Nowadays, Alex didn't even cross her mind when Cassie thought about Tyler's father. In every way except biologically, Adam was Tyler's dad.

They were so close, those two. Ty and his dad spent lots of happy times together, and not a day passed that Cassie didn't thank her lucky stars and a gracious God in heaven that Susan had forced her to look through that *Single Men of Alaska* magazine. It was definitely a blessing in disguise for all of them.

Speaking of Tyler's brilliant father, Adam had taken a full-time position at the new aquarium in Seward, overseeing all affairs from business—Adam hadn't mentioned that he had a minor in business, as well—to each animal's environment and food.

Looking around Adam's formerly spartan house now, she decided that she'd succeeded pretty well with their own environment. The feminine touches made a big difference. Even the table she'd set for their special lunch with her own pretty new china, a sunflower-printed tablecloth and napkins she'd made during a surge of energy one night when Adam was gone, added so much to the room.

Looking at the table with the salads she'd made already set out in serving bowls and the plump loaves of crusty brown bread just waiting to be cut, made her ravenous...not an uncommon occurrence lately.

Impatient for the fishing party to return not only because she was hungry, but because she was dying to make *the announcement,* she decided to walk the half mile down the road to the mailbox.

Cassie was staying as active as possible during her pregnancy because she knew it would make her delivery and recovery easier. She smiled her secret smile as she walked under a canopy of aspen trees, the smooth, round leaves flashing like silver dollars in the sun. It was the smile she'd been trying to hide ever since she got her ultrasound results late yesterday afternoon. Yes, she'd definitely need to be in good health come September.

Cassie opened the mailbox and was immediately assailed with the telltale scent of some exotic perfume. Pulling a thick stack of mail out, she knew what she'd find. Thumbing through bills and junk mail, she ran across the suspect envelope. It was powder-blue and addressed beautifully.

Yes, even after a year, replies to his *Single Men of Alaska* ad still came through. Cassie held the envelope near her nose and took a cautious sniff. That's what was stinking up the entire contents of the mailbox, all right.

Cassie admitted to a bit of jealous curiosity about the contents of these letters, and how they compared to her letter to Adam a year ago. But Adam had a very honorable method of handling his "fan mail." He sent them back unopened with a politely phrased apology printed neatly on the back, reading, "Thank you for your interest, but I'm happily married now. Good luck in your future endeavors. Adam Baranof."

Cassie knew that Adam was perfectly correct in handling the letters in this way, because it would be unkind to indulge their curiosity or entertain themselves at the expense of the letter writers. Cassie reminded herself of this as she firmly tucked this tempting morsel of a missive behind the stack she was sorting through, and found another interesting letter on top with international postmarks and colorful stamps. The return address was Brazil—it was a letter from Alex and Kelly.

With a quicker step, Cassie returned to the house just in time to meet the fishing party in the kitchen.

"Beautiful!" exclaimed Sylvie, her dark eyes sparkling, her cheeks glowing with health and happiness. "This state is *so* beautiful! And I've never seen so much wildlife. So many fish!"

"Sylvie, you just wait," Cassie warned her.

"You just got here. You haven't even scratched the surface of this incredible place."

She worked her way down the line of the three most important men in her life, all of them smelling of wind and water and just a teensy bit of fish.

She got on her tiptoes and kissed her father on the cheek. "Hi, Dad. Ummm. What's the after-shave?"

"It's called Fish Musk," he deadpanned, swatting her on the fanny as she passed.

She bent down to rub noses, Eskimo-style, with Tyler. It was a new thing with him. "You catch your limit, bud?"

"Not this time, Mommy." He leaned close to whisper, "I let Granddad catch the most 'cause he's a guest."

She laughed and tousled his dark hair. "Good sport, Ty."

Straightening up again, she found Adam waiting for her with open arms. Moving into that familiar yet always exciting embrace, they kissed with the restraint dictated by a roomful of people, but with tender looks that said much more.

"Feeling okay, hon?" he asked her.

"I feel fabulous."

"All ready for dinner?" He raised his brows in that particular way of his. A double meaning was implied and understood.

She smiled that secret smile. "Ready as I'll ever be."

"Did you get hold of Mom and Dad?"

"Yes. They'll be here in time for dessert. Your

dad couldn't get here sooner. He's coming between charters, meeting your mom at the docks.''

He nodded and they parted reluctantly. It was time to be host and hostess.

The men made quick work of cleaning the fish outside and Adam cooked them while Cassie passed out crackers, cheese and iced tea. Everyone was hungry. The great outdoors did that to you. So did pregnancy.

The meal was delicious, the conversation lively. When Cassie lifted the knife to cut the chocolate cake, the doorbell rang. Adam got up to let in his parents. There was general confusion as greetings were exchanged, then the group settled again in the living room with coffee and cake handed around by Adam and Cassie.

''Sit down, Cassie,'' Peter finally ordered as she started to collect empty plates. ''We should be waiting on you.''

Peter had proven to be a wonderful father-in-law, even a little protective. Monica was like a best friend.

''I can't sit still. I think I'm a little nervous,'' Cassie admitted, stealing a meaningful glance at Adam.

''Why are you nervous, sweetie?'' Jasper asked her, always alert to anything that might be amiss in his darling daughter's life.

Adam got up to stand next to his wife, his arm around her nonexistent waist as they faced the suddenly very attentive group. Even Tyler was bug-eyed as he sat happily squeezed between his two grandfathers.

"What's wrong, Mommy?" he demanded, not afraid to get right to the point.

"Nothing's wrong, Ty," Cassie told him. "Something's actually very, very right." She felt her eyes well with happy tears. She hated how easily she got emotional these days, but hormones usually had their way with you no matter what you tried to do about it.

Adam handed Cassie a handkerchief and asked a question with his eyes. She nodded. "What my wife is trying to tell you," he said at last, "is that she and I are the proud parents of twins."

"Twins? Well, I'll be damned!" Jasper declared.

Tyler was elated. "You mean I'm going to have two baby brothers! Wow!"

Peter exclaimed. "I can't believe it! Well...yes, I guess I can! I *should!*"

Monica was teary-eyed. "I'm so happy I could cry!"

"Lordy, girl, you're going to have your hands full! In a good way, of course. But *really* full." Sylvie concluded for everyone.

After the initial, spontaneous remarks were made, Adam's hand was pumped and they were both kissed to within an inch of their lives.

"Cassie, when did you find out?" Monica asked her as she wiped her eyes and blew her nose.

"Just yesterday afternoon. Believe me, I wouldn't hold out on you on something this important. We're both so excited!"

"If you wouldn't mind a little advice, I could tell you quite a bit about raising twins!"

"I know," Cassie said. "And I'm counting on

your sharing your wisdom. Only I think it might be a little bit different for me than it was for you."

"How's that?" Peter asked. "Believe me, Cassie, two boys the same age in the house is always a powder keg."

"That's the thing...." Cassie smiled down at Tyler and rested her hand on his head. "I hope you don't mind, Ty, but we're not getting two boys. We're getting a boy and a *girl*."

This caused another commotion that took some time to quiet down. By now Cassie was nearly exhausted from all the excitement. Seeing this, Adam made her sit down and gave everyone in the room a meaningful look. They quickly understood and bottled up their own excitement to explode like an uncorked champagne bottle at another location.

"We'd better go," Monica announced tactfully. "I have some errands to run and Peter has another charter in fifteen minutes. Don't you, dear?"

Peter followed his wife's lead and they were soon gone, smiling like lottery winners as they waved goodbye from the porch. Sylvie and Jasper left, taking Tyler with them for a walk into town. They looked like happy gamblers, too, so full of riches they could burst. Even Tyler was okay with the "girl" surprise. He was sure he could teach the female part of the pair to like fishing, too.

Left alone, Adam sat on an ottoman at the end of Cassie's chair and put her feet in his lap. He tenderly massaged her aching ankles and tired feet until Cassie thought she'd swoon from pleasure.

"Why are you so good to me?"

"Because I love you. And because you're the mother of my three children."

Cassie smiled. He always said the right thing.

Suddenly she remembered Alex's letter. Picking it up off a nearby table, she handed it to Alex. "All this talk of twins and I still forgot to tell you that you got a letter from your duplicate sibling."

He neatly opened the envelope with his thumbnail. "Shall I read it aloud?"

"Yes. Do. I want to hear how the happy couple likes Brazil."

Adam read the letter, which was written by Alex, the bulk of which was a vivid narration of their travels and activities for the past couple of weeks since leaving for Brazil from Florida to work for an oil company there for a few months. It all sounded so exciting, so adventurous, so perfect for Alex and Kelly. They were very happy together and very happy with their lives and jobs. It was again obvious to Cassie that Tyler was meant to be Adam's son, just as she was meant to be his wife.

"Listen to this, Cass," Adam said suddenly after puzzling over the last few sentences of the letter. "This is just too weird."

" 'Life is great, bro and Cass. I never thought I'd ever be this happy. But even more important to me is how happy you two are. Or should I say you four, counting my nephew, Ty, and the new little nephew you're carrying? Or is it *five*? Somehow, considering family patterns and all, I can't help thinking that maybe Cassie's carrying twins. But maybe heredity has nothing to do with it. Maybe when you're twice as deserving as the next couple, twice as nice, twice as happy as most, you get twice as many bundles of joy.'''

Cassie got teary-eyed again, grabbed a tissue, and mumbled defensively, "I can't help it. It's the hormones!"

Adam grinned and leaned forward to take his weeping wife in his arms. "It's okay, Cass. I'm happy enough to cry, too, and it's not hormones. *My* hormones are telling me to do something entirely different."

She smiled through her tears. "What's stopping you?"

He laughed. "Nothing," he said as he rested his hand on her stomach. "Nothing at all." Then he kissed her very tenderly on the lips.

HARLEQUIN®
AMERICAN ◆ ROMANCE®

*They're handsome, they're sexy, they're determined to remain single.
But these two "bachelors" are about to receive the shock of their lives...*

OOPS! STILL MARRIED!

August 1999—#787 THE OVERNIGHT GROOM
by Elizabeth Sinclair
Grant Waverly must persuade Katie Donovan to continue their newly discovered marriage for just two more intimate weeks....

September 1999—#790 OVERNIGHT FATHER
by Debbi Rawlins
Matthew Monroe never forgot the woman he'd once married for convenience. And now Lexy Monroe needs the man from whom she's kept one little secret....

Look for the special *Oops! Still Married!* duet, coming to you soon—only from Harlequin American Romance®!

The honeymoon is just beginning...

Available at your favorite retail outlet.

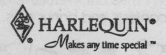

HARLEQUIN®
Makes any time special ™

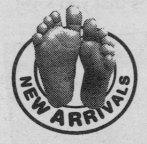

THE MACGREGORS OF OLD...

#1 *New York Times* bestselling author

NORA ROBERTS

has won readers' hearts with her enormously popular MacGregor family saga. Now read about the MacGregors' proud and passionate Scottish forebears in this romantic, tempestuous tale set against the bloody background of the historic battle of Culloden.

Coming in July 1999

REBELLION

One look at the ravishing red-haired beauty and Brigham Langston was captivated. But though Serena MacGregor had the face of an angel, she was a wildcat who spurned his advances with a rapier-sharp tongue. To hot-tempered Serena, Brigham was just another Englishman to be despised. But in the arms of the dashing and dangerous English lord, the proud Scottish beauty felt her hatred melting with the heat of their passion.

Available at your favorite retail outlet.

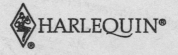

COMING NEXT MONTH

#785 THE LAST STUBBORN COWBOY by Judy Christenberry
4 Tots for 4 Texans
With his friends married and in a family way, Mac Gibbons thought the
bet was over, and he was safe from the matchmaking moms of Cactus,
Texas. That is, until he stopped to help a lady in distress and looked
down into the blue eyes of new doc Samantha Collins...and her baby
daughter. A daughter who looked amazingly just like Mac!

#786 RSVP...BABY by Pamela Browning
The Wedding Party
The last thing Bianca D'Alessandro needed was to be a bridesmaid at a
family wedding. Especially since she'd be bringing a pint-size guest no
one knew about. She could pass off the whispers, but she couldn't avoid
the best man, Neill Bellamy—the father of her secret baby....

#787 THE OVERNIGHT GROOM by Elizabeth Sinclair
Oops! Still Married!
Grant Waverly's career was his mistress...until he found out he
was married! Kathleen Donovan had been his one true love—and
apparently his wife for the past seven years, though neither one knew
it. But now that Grant had a wife, he intended to keep her!

#788 DEPUTY DADDY by Charlotte Maclay
Lawman Johnny Fuentes didn't know what to do with the beautiful
but very pregnant woman with amnesia who was found wandering in
town—except take her home. Trouble was, soon she began believing he
was her husband!

Look us up on-line at: http://www.romance.net